A HAPPY GHOST

Let me know what you think.
— Kristian

Kristian@alumni.usc.edu

KARL KRISTIAN FLORES

a happy ghost

A NOVEL

written in an apartment in westwood, california

www.karlkristianflores.com/books

Illustrated by Gigi Copeland
Edited by Candida Bradford
Publication Assembly by Surya Singh

to friends we walk
past & never meet.

CHAPTERS

LIST OF CHARACTERS *(in order of appearance)*

Andrei, *a young man*
The hotel manager, *chic and middle-aged*
Various hotel guests, *out of touch*
Mars, *an old woman*
Olivia, *a California native*
Stella, *a college student*
The San Francisco woman, *petite and in thirties*
David, *a young, enthused man*
The cashier, *a college-aged girl*
Stephanie, *tattoos, late 20s*
Elijah, *beard, mid-20s*
Lyn, *glasses, mid-20s*
Edgar, *weary, mid-30s*
The café worker, *thirty-two years old*
Jean, *early 20s*
Jean's date, *early 20s*
Ashu, *a lively woman in a hijab*
Lorenzo, *a handsome sound designer*
Amanda, *a troubled waitress*
The stranger not there, *an empty chair*
Bradford Keller, *a sharp agent*
The woman in green, *a Frenchwoman*
Chelsea, *an intern*
Brett, *a tall teenager*
A group of teenagers, *snobbish early teens*
Valet, *goofs*
A foodrunner, *an energetic kid*
A stern guard, *tall and stiff*
A college couple, *naked*
Alejandra, *a sweet scholar*
A mother, *hurt*
A son, *passionate and evil*
A sister, *sorrowful and trying*
A poet, *awkward*
Raphael, *a funny boy who wears gray*
Dr. O'Hare, *a professor*
Various students, *a new generation*
The pale man, *shirtless and early thirties*
A mother by the bus stop, *Hispanic*
Noelle, *small*
Michael, *large*
Officer Gonzales, *a pianist*
Officer Villalobos, *an influencer*
Forty candles, *lighted*
A classroom of kids, *youthful and playing*
The happy ghost, *Andrei*

HAPPY GHOST

hello. i am dead, very dead—in case you wondered who was going to narrate this story. how are you? if you thought, 'good,' i wish you more of that. if you thought 'bad,' i'm sorry but give me a chance and soon you will be better. me? death is a charm. my experience is an interminable glaze of beauty, with inklings of infinite reflections from my past life, nebulae, and stars. sometimes, i laugh even with nothing to laugh at. i do not actually *think*—instead my spirit seems to drift in every direction, blurrily, without a care, but ultimately content because it came from earth, which while quite hellish, actually digests as something impossibly delightful! and every now and then, i gather a few words and string them together. if i were to calculate, time passes at about nine thousand five hundred ninety-six years for every word i create for this book. the writing takes a while, but i don't really mind. time is all i have. yes, we write after we die. it seems the need to create had nothing to do with a desperation to understand oneself during our aliveness, but rather the discharge of natural, tiny volumes of our soul. here comes six bubbles:

there

was

a

boy

named:

andrei.

I

THE BEDROOM

"*C*ome on, dream…" he dreamed.

Andrei's room was as still as a photograph. Air did not pass through. Not over the thin glass of leftover merlot staining the ground with a perfect circle beside his futon mattress that, too, laid flat on the cold hardwood floor. Not over the boy asleep who wished to dream and failed.

It smelled of earth and mushroom, coming from the half-eaten rind of camembert melted on his nightstand. The ivory black paint on his wall, self-done, had given his room calm. A heavy, gold clock hoisted above his desk displaying a sheet of glass that slowly glared hotter and hotter. The reflection, that covered time's hand, came from the awaking sun, which eagerly arrived every morning in front of the building's stained-glass windows. But then within time, whenever that was, a cloud would push daylight away and the day would become gray.

Andrei's sparse collection of clothing hung on handcrafted wooden hangers—a black puffer jacket, a suit, two dress shirts, a brown coat, and a university hoodie. The puffer jacket did not suit Los Angeles' dry climate. The brown coat was adorned because of its many pockets. And the university hoodie was fraudulent, as its owner had never attended college. He only wore it to fit in the neighborhood of

Westwood, living so close to the prestigious school that partied outside his dark window every night. Andrei would rather people not know he'd barely graduated from continuation high school and never pursued an ambitious career. His unsuccessful face, according to an awakened him, was "the kind that people see trouble in." However, when he wore a blue hoodie with "UCLA" beautifully inscribed in yellow cursive, he could walk into libraries and parking garages without suspicious looks or outright accusations.

On his desk was an array of worn-out novels and works of non-fiction in especially terrible condition. One of the books even looked burnt, and others seemed to have survived a day in the ocean to be dried out in the sun. If one saw Andrei's little library, they would wonder how the hell some books could get so damn ugly.

His toes rubbed against each other, like tiny chicks rubbing their necks on their siblings, and Andrei felt himself waking.

He yawned, his face performing that universal mixture of a smile and a frown as he stretched his arms out. One was not sure why faces did this—either waking people were activating their muscles in preparation for the day or more soulfully, the smile was gratitude for life and the frown to follow was recognition of what that life entailed.

But soon, always soon, Andrei's pale face would reveal his soul: motionless. Few things could excite a movement in him, not even a loud sound. His eyelids drooped the same way his cheeks sunk, low and hushed. He ran his hand through the curls of his brown hair and rubbed his purple blanket against his lips. He listened to the ticking sounds of his watch and, after a few minutes, got up for work, walked mindlessly down the street, and found himself in that familiar hotel lobby.

"Good afternoon, front desk. Andrei speaking. How can I—fuck!"

The greasy phone slipped out of Andrei's hands.

"Sorry about that. How can I assist you?" asked Andrei. "Hello?"

"What kind of shit show do you think you're running?" yelled the guest.

"I apologize, sir," said Andrei nervously. "The phone slipped from my hands and it's my first day." Andrei had been working here for three and a half years.

"The what?" asked the guest. "No. There's a cockroach in my fucking room. And there's blood on the bed sheets. Hold on—wait a second. Right there on the wall, is that… is that a booger? Christ! Where am I?"

Andrei took vigorous notes. "Sir, I apologize for the… cockroach… the blood… and…the… the booger. Got it."

"Are you writing this down?"

"Um, no."

"Well you fucking should be, dumbass. I'm a crown member of this hotel. Isn't this supposed to be Beverly Hills?"

The floor manager of the Beverly Hills property of cockroaches, blood, and boogers approached the desk, listening carefully. His ears, pierced at the lobe in silver, leaned toward his employee. The manager, wearing his usual eyeliner, and pink blush, calmly searched Andrei's face for trouble.

"Yes, sir. We are in Beverly Hills," Andrei said, sensing his manager. "Is there anything else I can assist you with?"

"This is a terrible hotel."

"The pleasure is mine, sir. We'll get right to it!"

"Get right to fucking what?"

"No worries at all. Welcome in, sir. Enjoy the rest of your stay!"

"I want a room upgrade!"

"You too," said Andrei.

And he hung up. Andrei's pleased manager nodded in approval. Before his way to his office, the manager handed Andrei a list of room numbers intended for amenity deliveries. If a hotel guest had chosen to stay at the property in celebration of an anniversary or birthday, the staff would present them with a bottle of alcohol, usually gin or vodka. Six anniversaries and two birthdays were occurring that day.

Andrei should have grabbed a bellman's cart to support the run, but instead carried eight shining bottles firmly tucked under his arms, all equidistant to each other, pressed against his chest which was sprayed with the hotel's signature cobalt scent. He kept his shelf-like form and the bottles were ready for choosing. To his thinking, the physical effort of his amenity delivery would prevent complaints. Presentation, he'd learned, meant more to the world than he thought. Guests complained about the most seemingly minor things: the location of lamps, the creases on a couch, the mechanics of a window, and even the room number. It bothered Andrei, but not because he despised the guest's standards of living. More so his disappointment came from speculating that a stranger's preferences, so felt and specific, could never be foreseen.

There were always difficult guests. Though for the most part, people delighted to be away from home and entered the hotel in awe of its décor, music, and seduction. When Andrei checked guests in, they would talk sweet and appear easygoing, but within days, he would pick up the phone and learn more about their tastes. Those personalities he met during their check-in never reappeared. Instead, he was met with agonizing demands and uncivil attitudes. The guest's minute requests led to Andrei's newfound, quiet distrust for human beings. He was afraid of how much people actually cared about things—from feather pillows to spinach. He felt naïve to where people paid their attention. Everyone had their own right to like and dislike certain things, but he found it eerily strange that people behaved warmly with their friends and family. If, however, they were speaking to a concierge, a chef, or a server, more honest sentences were spoken. Andrei's fool was extinguished. He learned that everyone's strongest observations and preferences were concealed until a telephone appeared at their bedside that was open to their complaints. So while the introductions to these humans were amicable, their repressed disapprovals were endless and their detailed detestation for any infraction was cocked and ready to fire.

Do people really like the way they're fucked? he thought. *Do wives like their husband's faces? Does my weak vocabulary annoy these intelligent CEOs? How long can I speak until I bother someone? They will all smile and shake your hand, but I am afraid I am just another omelet missing the ingredient they want. I am the wrong piano key fiercely played by a pianist's regretful pinky finger in a concert hall blaring false to the audience's disturbed ears that certainly caught the note but whose controlled heads do not dare betray their feigned enjoyment.* He felt all this in the ascending, disco-lit elevator towering its way up to the skies of West Los Angeles. Andrei made his rounds.

The first door he delivered to opened with the slightest angle. "Happy Bir—." A quick, bony hand shot out to grab the neck of the bottle and closed the door. *thday.*

The second door he knocked on did not open. Andrei heard no sound inside, so he left the bottle outside on the floor.

The third door presented a man in gym attire. The man wearing turquoise shorts frowned at Andrei and waited, wondering who was obligated to break the silence. Andrei's smile gestured to the alcohol and the birthday guest said, "Er—thanks."

The fourth door was opened by a slender lady in a bathrobe, who giggled and said, "You didn't have to, handsome! I love your hair! I will tip you when I go out later!"

The fifth door was opened by a chubby little boy, maybe eight or nine years old, who took the alcohol and told Andrei in a deep voice that imitated the child's father: "Appreciate you."

The sixth door was opened by a tall, old man with glasses, who asked in a British accent: "Who the fuck drinks Grey Goose?"

The seventh door opened to a younger, wide-eyed gentleman who licked the inside of his cheek and blinked rapidly while Andrei gave his spiel. The guest fidgeted on his feet and sniffed occasionally. Once he took the amenity, he grabbed the back of Andrei's neck, pulled him forward, and thanked him. The guest then reached into his pocket and with rough, sloppy hands placed a generous amount of cash in Andrei's hands.

The eighth door slowed Andrei's heart. Out came an older lady, with marks of two dried rivers on her face. She looked at Andrei's brown eyes and after a tiny burst of a tearful hiccup, solemnly said in broken English, "This...exactly... what I needed honey... Thank you." She smiled, then closed the door. Andrei was moved and, feeling both pity and curiosity, knocked on her door again. She answered, her face holding no trace of surprise. This woman understood souls well enough to know a soft one would return. And the soft one did. He sat by her bed, and without either of them saying a word, they held each other for minutes. He got up, left, and heard her open the bottle before the door closed.

The world varies. That was what he realized in the hallway. Eight doors—all so different. Some answered, some didn't. Some smiled, others were gruff. Compliments could arise right before a harsh rejection. One must never settle on a perspective. A perspective implied an agreement of what a day can be—be it sunny or sorrowful—but one could not trust in the hopes, hazards, and scope of what a day entailed. The possibilities of who one met were endless and people encountered in a day changed too quickly. In order to grasp the chaos of the day, the brain may want to cling to a principle, but the understandings they carried were limited solely to that brain's interactions. Thus, for humans, most of whom hardly live in their waking hours, attaining a virtuous life was a numbers game— a series of saints and demons is what freed the mind. But if one could not experience a thousand goods and bads in an afternoon, they must imagine these experiences. This recalibrates extreme emotions or interpretations of any kind. A sad day was not worth surrendering to because it only meant the depressed heart had not seen enough. A happy day was not worth believing because it had not yet reached the night. There was no single weather for humans. One must accept all, precisely because there were those eight doors. When this indifference swirled in his head, a neutral smile curled up on Andrei's lips. This acceptance was like dessert.

He entered the elevator.

It was best to follow nothing, neither optimism nor pessimism. Everyone wanted to be one or the other: happy or upset. But if one committed to truth, living attentively to fleeting moments, shaking loose of generalizations of templates and premonitions, life promised great joy. The joy from this is impossible to casually share with a person who asks, "How are you?" The person who held the truth would not make sense. But that is the trade-off. The world did not welcome people who tried to understand it.

To be clear, Andrei pursued truth, but he suffered terribly. It was not pain that tortured him, but a question. This question was not of melancholy tone or negative spirit—but a burning dissatisfaction. He longed to rationalize a way out of his monotony. The question that was buried deep within Andrei, that emerged in his voice, his wishing eyes, and movements of his hands was: *what is there?* A profound boredom in him was his chief concern.

The elevator dropped to the twelfth floor.

The hourly pay of the hotel gig was generous. It gave him time and options. Andrei had enough money to try every genre of food there was in the city, as well as their subcategories. He had delighted in the freshest toro handrolls, tastiest racks of lamb that a visiting international chef could present, and purest cabeza tacos available. He would feel the need to treat himself when a day was hard, but found that every day was hard and so treated himself every day. He had also taken multiple trips to galleries, landmarks, zoos, and museums. He dedicated weeks alone in his room listening to some of the most important music albums ever made. He watched movies at double speed—adjusting the play settings of a film in order to quickly watch the next. And afterward, that question dawned on him like a mocking shadow. *What is so interesting about this place?* he thought gently. He was not asking about the meaning of life. His conflict was not existential, but a practical plea. There was no fury in the man, rather a hollow aching whose sound would be closest to a polite cry.

Everything was predictable. Cinema had act structures. Music had beats. Poets had tricks. Books had arcs. Food tasted delicious as long as it was on the surface of one's tongue. Any chance of happiness was but one single carousel round, so naturally, after a while, the passenger felt expired. To Andrei, there ceased to be anything worth chasing and this feeling of "running out" in an abundant globe confused him. He wished there was something in the world that was infinite or lasted forever—or was at least worth remembering forever. This was why the sleeper could not dream—his imagination writhed in his true-to-life gluttony.

Eleventh floor.

Of course, there were experiences he'd never had. He had never dived from a cliff, nor had he ever gotten lucky with a girl in a sports car going a hundred miles per hour in Italy. But to him, once he did things, they got done, and that was the end. Cliff diving and steamy scenic routes become the same experience once one unlocked its program: adrenaline and excitement. Then, they mattered as much as any little thing that gave him a dose of energy. *Experience is simply a mantra we say to ourselves to keep us from hearing the actual song of life—which is the beating heart of a soul unsure of why it is here,* thought Andrei. *Place a hand on the heart of one nearby, feel it pounce, listen, and all at once, their achievements go away and they are the same as you.*

Tenth floor.

He held envy for bodies that found fulfillment in something like a morning hike, family time, or even engaging in an art like sculpture. But these activities had no layer of infinity underneath. Even the desire to enjoy a meal with someone was broken in him—cracked not from tragedy, but witness. Nothing goes far. He watched the arc of social gatherings from the hotel. Andrei positioned himself near affluent dinner parties to eavesdrop on the wealthy, often famous. After this study, he knew firsthand that no group was exempt from the awkwardness of conversation. Greatness was a façade. Because every one of those dinners, no matter how smart the table was, started out with the impressive walk from valet to the booth, followed by the applause of each other's shiny dresses, but the food came and the evening turned out to be as ordinary as a suburban family dinner.

The rich used to be up in the hills, but now he was too. This reality was a hard hole to crawl out of—mainly because this hole did not have a definitive light above in which to toil toward. There was only the dark and ash and puddles.

Ninth floor.

This hole, from an outside eye, was most clear on his days off from work. In that period, it looked how it was— beginning with loose tea leaves and a cinnamon cookie. Then he read, played his maple acoustic guitar, looked at old photos, stared at passersby, and saw that it was still only eleven o'clock in the morning.

Andrei was in an elusive period in life, much like a snow leopard. He'd spent a couple of years having successfully filtered out all that was terrible and ugly in his life, from old shoes to lifeless people. However, the purification finished and he had not yet found the glint of gold to replace the damned. He had nowhere to place his lifted foot. Instead, his moral foot hovered, awkwardly, a crepuscular flesh, trembling every night, unable to set itself in a correct place. He lived in that hanging imbalance every day, and some would say this period of searching takes a while. But to him, all it did was take. Not a while. The peace of his life just takes. And takes. And takes. While Andrei may not suffer from the heat of stress or common negativity that improperly placed feet do, he lived cold, in a void, without the luxury of finding a worthy arrangement for his leopard paw.

Eighth floor.

For many years, video games gave him a person and a place to be, as well as things to do. But an event happens to a pair of eyes after enough hours before a computer screen— they will scan the display and mid-game, shatter. Consoles crack men. It's massacre. Andrei would thumb plastic so often that his mind would flee reality, as well as the virtual world he was in, and enter a dimension of empty euphoria. But one euphoric day he felt games were a sophisticated way to keep a pig in its own corner. The videogames advanced to become more realistic—but one must not be fooled by decorations. The detail-rich galaxies he found himself investing his life in were in fact the same galaxy as Pacman or Tetris: 1s and 0s.

Seventh floor.

Pornography did not serve him either. Andrei used to have his personal kinks and fetishes, but after a while, nothing could get him off. For a long time, the only videos he would search were the ones titled: "Who is she?" The only thing that vitalized his self-play was the prospect of some woman on the earth no one knew of and could not find. There was something infinite to these tapes, not the appearance of the girls, but the agitating dissatisfaction and momentary access of a not-so-innocent stranger who men innocently lost forever. It consisted of poorly recorded videos, posted from a smartphone or webcam, and a desperate number of melancholy comments trying to search for the mystery woman. There were plenty of these recordings. But it broke

Andrei even more when eventually he knew all the girls no one knew.

He could take a walk, or enjoy more of a dead person's art, but this would not solve the problem begging to be calculated in himself: *what is there?*

Sixth floor.

Whenever he contemplated death, he felt he would miss thinking most of all. There was a delicate pleasure of thought and sensation. The awareness of it. The inner voice of thoughtless reasoning, effortless analyzing, ceaseless tingling. It was the only thing a person had if everything were taken away from them. It was what continued to exist before they touched any object or heard any sound once awaken from slumber. That personal conversation was irreplaceable. Andrei would be upset at death, whenever it came, because of what it entailed: no longer being able to look down and see one's hands. No longer being able to feel a breathing belly. No longer able to wonder, or to remember a memory. It surprised him, in such a stupid, sad way, that there was no save button in life. *Yes, yes, we die, I get it,* he thought, but for some reason, he'd pathetically assumed he could take something with him. That death would be okay because at least he would still be able to reflect. In theory, he would die and get to say, *"Whew, I died. Now let's think about it."* But he wouldn't. All the memories he had earned would wash away instantly. The work done on oneself could not be transferred. He would not trim his fingernails or have the chance to check out another woman's ass ever again. Death was flat. Aliveness had texture. But even though Andrei knew he would miss life, it did not change the irrefutable reality that there was nothing to do in it.

Fifth floor.

He did not want to write a book about it. He'd tried once, attempting a novel, even some poems, but they broke his heart and he could not bring himself to art anymore. *So the only way to end this painful curiosity is to transfer it to someone else? To fictionalize it? To talk about it and still live*

23

the same problem tomorrow? To appear as if you've beaten it just because you can identify the problem? He would sob in museums, where he sought refuge but escaped in horror. *Fuck that—art's not an answer to life, it's a disguise. And if it's not a disguise, then someone else has already said it before so there's no need to add to the library.* In addition to this scorn, he could not stand being called a writer. Andrei had seen writers attend conference summits before. Their stories were fantastic, but their real voices were dull and they had these reptilian eyes that looked at people like they were going to put them in their book. One novelist had seemed as if she lived in a refrigerator somehow. He watched them robotically discuss the key to successful storytelling and since then, he'd never trusted artists. They were awkward liars. How could he depend on their ideas? How could he place his faith and meaning in lifeless people like that? And again, the scorn would resurface and he would despise what writing a book meant for himself: that whenever he had a concern, the only way out was to turn it into an idea. Art was treated merely as company to the misunderstood artist who mistook fame for understanding. *No, not me. I will never replicate life to seem above it. I will be under it, beneath its heavy force, smaller, underground—a worm.*

Andrei theorized that the predicament of tedium a realized mind finds itself in is of human territory. Being a conflict exclusive to his species, any solution implied that to break out of the problem of malaise was to become something different altogether. Precisely, non-human. That was what he searched for and would try to find. This did not mean any kind of supernatural metamorphosis—but rather a way out of himself and all selves.

Fourth floor. Someone entered the elevator.

"Oh, hi, excuse me, where are your ice machines?"

"Our ice machines are on every floor, ma'am."

"Even on the fourth floor?"

"Yes, right there."

"Are you sure?"

"Would you like me to show you?"

"Sure!"

Andrei walked a few feet down the corridor and pointed at the room with the ice machine. The lady, who had remained by the elevator, watched him from afar.

"Ah! Thank you!" And completely forgetting where they'd met, she stepped back and let the elevator doors close between them.

As Andrei stood alone in the middle of the hallway, he heard a pounding to his left, behind a guest's door. He leaned his ear in closer and listened as a woman moaned in rhythm. Seconds later, she asked to be slapped.

She must be something, he thought. *Who can scream the way she does? So loud and free?* But then his stomach grew dark, aching at the sign of some other man giving her pleasure. *What makes the man inside so worthy?* he asked himself. But he pressed his face against the door and continued listening. Her noises grew so intense Andrei pressed his lips against the door, closed his eyes, and could not help the bulge beneath his belt buckle growing hotter by the minute. He could hear the man breathe inside, whispering something to the woman. *What's he saying?* Andrei grew ever more curious.

He walked to the office door parallel to the elevators and checked the clipboard which listed the housekeeping status of each floor. *425.* This room to the right of the noises was listed as vacant-clean. Andrei took out his keys and, drawn by a passionate need, entered the suite.

He rushed to the minibar and grabbed the rocks glass stacked on the top of the pyramid, placed it on the wall, and lifted his ear against the cold cup echoing his neighbor's fuck.

More slapping ensued. The woman's voice belted in a vibration of pleasure and exhaustion. It was the scream a woman screams that says: "Oh god!" and gets muffled when a hand is placed over her mouth that wants more. The man moaned too. Andrei imagined him pulling her hair and at the assumption of that sight, dropped his own pants and began to touch himself. The lady would scream and Andrei would respond in dialogue as if it was just him and her. He kissed the wall and bent his knees. For an instant, he grew ashamed and sad. He himself was not touched very often. Andrei sensed how pathetic he must have looked, but he was much too lonely to care. He sped up and could feel the devil cheering, "Lower. Go as low as hell," and he limboed his way into that hell. And it was freezing and it was hot. One knows they are truly gone when their own tears start to lubricate their self-play. Andrei kept going, stroking wet, painfully, finishing at the same time the man did. And then the door opened.

2

THE QUEEN SUITE

Andrei pulled his pants up as quietly as he could and hid in the closet. He was covered in shame.

Behind the white blinds, he watched his newest guest turn the corner and roll a designer suitcase toward her bed. Andrei held his breath while she unpacked.

Her hands were not the hands one thought would come attached to the wrists they saw, to the body they saw, to the face they saw. Her wrists were thin, wrinkled, and had gold bracelets worn like favorites. Her limber body swayed as though in time to an orchestra and in a way that showed she ate well, and ate all kinds of things no one could tell, like veal or fresh figs in the sunshine.

She had the kind of face that made one cry. Lucky people who studied the woman without her noticing were themselves moved to tears just by that face. She drew salt water out like sheer chemistry. The chemical reaction was usually the same sentiment—the world saw the little shelf bone under her eyes, a sharp nose, precious jaw, two moons for cheekbones, and so was deeply confused and upset that there was no metal armor attached to her body to protect her. The old lady deserved an astronaut suit at least. People had cried fearing all kinds of possibilities—that a piece of hail might cut across her cheek, a drunkard might break her nose, or a car from nowhere would crash into hers and shatter her skull entirely. But no case of that happened. She remained unblemished. Watchful cars slowed down for her as she walked, drunkards sobered at her eyes, and even hail made way for this little human. Those blessed persons who got to see her in their lifetime suddenly understood why war was evil. Looking at Mars, that was her name, they grew protective of humanity. They even understood by looking at her the reason fathers kiss the top of their daughters' heads, placing their lips on furry hair in a deep pucker that says, "Let no harm touch the surface of this circular, bone dome of yours. So I'll kiss it. Have a safe day, my girl."

That was her face, her wrists, her body. But her hands were manly. Not in size, but texture. They were rough and stubby—lost of all grace in such a depleted fashion one wondered if it had ever been there in the first place. They tanned too, hideously tawny above her veins, and seemed overworked. Later Andrei would grasp how perfectly this fit her. How a beautiful woman whose hands died beautiful lived stuck in a gorgeous shell and never knew about anything but gorgeous shells. People like Mars, however, he would learn, were precious gems that toiled through harsh years to make diamonds of their own.

Mars' ugly hands stroked the walls. It was a ritual she liked to host in every room once alone.

She noticed a glass cup on the floor. Mars took the glass, held her ear against its base to the wall and smiled as the neighbors went for a second round. The bed rocked, but the couple was quiet.

"Lift her leg, baby," said Mars.

And once spoken, as if instructions the strangers could hear, a powerful scream of pleasure ignited on the third floor.

"Good," smiled Mars.

Before she turned, Mars saw a drop of semen drawing its plot down the wall. She calmly put down the cup, faced the closet, and said, "If you can hand me a towel, sweetie."

Andrei froze. *Is the talking to me?* No one said anything. *Yes, she is. No. There's no chance. She can't be. She's on the phone.*

"If you think I'm on the phone, I'm not. I'm talking to you. A towel would be so nice," she said.

Does she know I'm in the closet?

"You're in the closet. You probably have something of your own to clean up, so feel free to take a shower," she said, eyeing a stranger's pair of keys on the coffee table.

Andrei gulped. He stepped out and, in a panic, mumbled, "Ma'am I am so sorry—please, just please, I'm a pervert, I know—"

"Oh god, stop it—"

"I'm—"

"Stop it! I would've done the same thing. You're not in trouble. What am I, your boss?"

"No."

"Right, so go ahead and clean this up. Or you're fired." She beamed with flirty eyes that waited impatiently for a witty follow-up or better yet, the same eyes.

"Okay," he let her down.

While Andrei wiped his shame clean off the wall, Mars unpacked her beauty products.

Sweat came over Andrei's eyes. His face burned and blood flooded his head so loudly his eardrums cracked. He leaned on the wall to breathe. All the while, Mars went around the room as if the scene was what ordinarily happened in hotel rooms. Her calmness bewildered him.

"Do you want me to go?" said the boy.

Mars looked at him in her languid sensuality. He was panting.

"'Cause I can go!"

"Well, why don't you? You obviously want to stay. What are you looking to figure out?"

And once again she did it, like in the closet—completing his thoughts and saying what he could not say out loud. He was so bothered by her doing this, but was so impressed that he conquered his fear to ask:

"How do you say what you say? How do you say what I'm thinking?"

"Everyone thinks the same thing. You just have to catch the thought right away before it turns into something else."

We think the same thing? How is that possible when there is so much disagreement? thought Andrei. He wanted to question the woman further, but as much as he needed to dream in his sleep again, he was too afraid to look like a person in need of a question answered. His front desk agent impulses reacted.

"What brings you to Los Angeles?" he asked professionally. She sensed his artificiality.

"I was born here. I'm an actress," she said.

"Oh, wow! Anything that I've—" And then it hit him. Andrei knew her face from somewhere. He did not have too large of an investment in the film industry to know actresses' names, but he recognized her.

Andrei swallowed his sentence and nodded politely. The lady continued to unpack. Her ease seemed to transfer onto him. His heart slowed and once calm, a genuine question bubbled to the surface.

"What's it like to be an actress?"

Oh god, thought Andrei. *I just came all over her wall and now I'm asking about her career. What am I thinking?* He began to panic again, unsure of himself.

Mars held her clothes up in the air and slipped them onto hangers. "It's a beautiful thing to be in Hollywood... the feeling of it... that classical glamour never dies." She walked to the closet and back to the bed. She liked the question. She used to think about it every day. "The actress lives a beautiful life once at a certain level... when her sink has a view and her phone calls aren't rejections anymore, but producers, offices, playhouses in London, a director pitching his sacred screenplay. The food gets healthier, people around you are more positive... driving in traffic is even different because your car is nice, and the music you normally hate sounds different when life works... when you get the furniture you want... And mentors pass down movie posters from *their* mentors—so Hepburn never really dies. You keep it in your home... there's room for everything... I treasure letters from other artists... studio invitations... Being a woman in Hollywood is entirely different than a man's experience. All the time, by everyone, for everything, a woman is wanted... dinners... so many dinners... so many scripts lying around the room, in the sun... the people you have yet to meet... it's not about fame—I do not care for the public praise... but what is truly compelling is when you make it big, you finally understand why there are palm trees in this city... Los Angeles suddenly turns on. Like a bulb you thought disliked you and would never light. But it lights. Of course, one must put the cocktail down, leave the house, and make more movies. But this is to say, the after hours are nice. When the camera is off and I return home, I get to love what is left."

She looked at the enchanted Andrei who saw Hollywood's eternal allure. Mars eyed his chocolate hair, then made her way a little down, to his brutish eyes, which were shaped in a way that meant, sadly, most people he met in life would never understand him. They were like eyeballs placed in two slits on his face that made him look distrustful. It required fifteen to thirty total hours of eye contact to understand Andrei. And in a conversation, the average eye contact added up to no more than thirty seconds. But when one did reach that lofty mark and kept with him, Andrei would tell when they now looked *in* him— and there would forge an unbreakable loyalty between them so golden, those friendly eyes would love the boy no matter if they ever saw him again.

But if there was anything to combat those fifteen to thirty hours, it would be a woman close to a century in age, who had seen parts of eyes like his in different people, and knew him for who he was, even if he did not yet know who he was. She saw a strange, dark greatness in him—dark not out of evil, but because it was hidden so far into him. She tried to pull it out.

"You seem desperate for something. For some kind of answer."

"Yes."

"Tell me what it is."

The air conditioning rumbled above them. It was a beautiful suite—a pool view, spacious bar and living area, and one of the few rooms that had a deep-soaking tub.

"I am numb to life," Andrei heard himself say.

To speak the words out loud, having lived so long and silently in him, gave him a shock. Mars was patient. He regained himself and continued: "I'm trying to find a reason to enjoy the day. I don't think there is anything here."

"Oh. So it's that kind of pain."

"Do you know it?" His voice almost cracked. "Um, but," he said, embarrassed at his desperation, "it's not pain. It's boredom."

"But it hurts… doesn't it?" said Mars.

"Yes. It hurts. It hurts to feel the same. Sameness."

She sat on the crisp white bed that yawned the special scent of fresh sheets.

"What do you wear on your days off?"

"This. Maybe a sweater."

"How do you know how you are if you wear the same things as before?" she asked. Mars had the gift of being able to illustrate a point with the wildest connections. She could prove a murder case by relating it to orange peels or could bring out secrets in someone by comparing plant species. She never explained the same thing twice and her examples were as fresh as the others. Truth worked that way. Honesty could take any shape—innumerably—but when a lie was released, no matter how creatively fabricated, it was stiff and finite. "Same outfits, same person," she said. "You have to shake your life until you rid yourself of everything you thought you were. You will shiver during the transition and then replenish with non-identity. After that, you'll see clearly. What does that mean? Well, you may have to move out of this country. Build your closet from the ground up. Befriend those you despise. Take a left. Trade different things, you see? One must refresh themselves. Stay current with the needs of our soul."

"The adventure isn't real though… like, people don't actually do those things. It's very romantic, but it's not true. People don't actually do that."

"What in the world? Do you know your history? We are anything– *anything*!—we are… in medieval times, kings would behead their brothers. Rulers would commission the most talented artists in the world to paint their bathroom ceilings. People have defeated mammoths with sticks. People have loved. People have killed the innocent to hurt the guilty. Waited until dawn. Mocked death. Staged coup d'états. Go further in your emotions and convictions. Increase your tolerance for extremity. Life can stretch."

"I think you're mad," giggled Andrei, shifting his feet.

"Like a comet," she stared with a firm jaw. Her seriousness skewered Andrei's comfort and he was unable to match her intensity.

"I… gotta go down now. Thank you. Enjoy your stay." He caught a glimpse of her hands. "And about earlier…" he said, looking at the wall.

"See. You've already started."

They shared a glow in each of their eyes, a gleam of light that acknowledged that these past ten minutes were some they would not dare utter to a soul, though would preserve with great care. Andrei went down the fire escape and took the stairs so he could reflect on the lady for longer. *I did not even catch her name*, he thought.

When Andrei reached the lobby, he ran into a long-term guest, Mr. Cohen, who was residing at the hotel for four pleasurable months. He greeted Andrei cheerfully. Andrei shook the man's hand, remembering all the nice compliments the guest had given him on the first day they met:

"You are so welcoming. Very rare to meet staff like you. I'm going to tell your manager about you. Thank you so much for making my stay so great! You're just so good! My favorite part about this place!"

While flattering, Andrei had since found it uncomfortable each time the grateful guest walked past his reception area. Andrei had run out of kind sentiments to reciprocate to Mr. Cohen authentically and could not keep up with the number of times they'd crossed each other, crossings where merriment was expected. When bumping into Mr. Cohen, who praised the front agent so highly, Andrei was unable to be anything else. His voice was set so high it nearly always cracked. When Mr. Cohen and Andrei first met, Andrei helped find the perfect room for him. The two toured different rooms, had great laughs, and looked forward to his upcoming stay. They bonded naturally, like brothers. But then Mr. Cohen began commending Andrei's duty and there formed an awkward expectation to uphold. The initial brotherhood never was the same once both parties said out loud how much they enjoyed the other. They got stuck at the greeting. The guest and agent did not want to hurt or offend the other person in a way that impacted their bond. They could not get anywhere further than their flashing teeth competing against each other. "I'm more happy to see you! Know that!" their smiles said.

As they shook hands, Andrei and Mr. Cohen looked at each other for an extra-long second, but no words came out. Both of them were waiting on the other to speak but were in fact thinking: "There's the fella I like. He likes me! Let's keep it that way… why isn't he saying anything? I can't keep this up." And smiling again, while feeling that uncomfortable, shapeless compromise between them, they waved goodbye to each other.

"The best, bro!" said Mr. Cohen, shouting across the lobby.

"No, that's you, Mr. Cohen!"

Why say it, Mr. Cohen? Dammit? Why'd you say it! The pressure! You pinned me! We can't move anymore! thought Andrei. *Sometimes you must arrest the tongue to let your heart run free.*

Mr. Cohen took the elevator up to his room and scratched his beard. He heard a fictitious note in Andrei's voice just then. *Weird.* The guest wondered if he had said something wrong to the boy. Or done something. *No. I told him he was great,* thought Mr. Cohen. *He had to know!*

3

GAYLEY AVENUE

T he hotel manager squirted a spray of blue liquid over the credit card machines and wiped them down with a cloth. He scrubbed at the number pads and turned his head toward the approaching heel clicks.

"Ah. Thank you for a good day, Andrei," waved the hotel manager.

"Goodbye," said Andrei, who looked down at his manager's white, crocodile leather shoes, and left.

He punched out of work and made his way back home. Normally, he rode his bicycle, but ever since some day or other, he'd started to walk. There was no reason for this. He simply wanted to walk and no longer take his bicycle. It was the same way he slept on the floor some nights, bought brown eggs instead of white, tried eating with chopsticks, and walked backward to work.

He hated walking. It was the most excruciating activity in his day; that was, because of the screaming. You see, passing strangers on a walk is terribly painful for people like Andrei, whose every muscle fights to pretend their mind is not yelling questions like: "DO YOU GO LEFT?! OR DO I? Do I know you? Are you looking at me? Do I look familiar to you? Look down! Peruse the floor, scan left now right. Where

36

are your headphones? It would have been so much easier to look busy if you had just remembered to bring your headphones! They're coming closer. Don't look at them. Rub your eyes. Sniffle. Good. Good…We made it. OH GOD ANOTHER ONE."

It was said that walking cleared the mind, but all it did was convolute Andrei's. There was nothing relaxing about walking. It was as if the ordinary movement of two legs was an outward ceremony for the world to hide the pink, uncontrollable machine thinking monstrous thoughts and concealing monstrous thoughts.

He paced home with his arms hanging awkwardly at his side. Andrei tried to look natural. *Put your arms like this,* he said to himself. *And swing them according to each step.* But his effort to be like everyone else only made him appear an alien stuck in a man's body. He admired folks that could effortlessly stroll around Westwood Village. Those young men and women looked like they had it all. *How the hell,* Andrei thought, *did they reach that place without getting trapped and stuck in this irritable reality I find myself in?* His life was equivalent to a pinball machine, his soul the last ball, and that ball going straight down into the depths of everything that sucked.

A man, perhaps an inch shorter than Andrei, sensing the height comparison, slowly passed him. The stranger still wore an N-95 mask. The pandemic ended three years ago, but Andrei identified why masks were still worn by others. While millions had died from COVID-19, others silently and ashamedly rejoiced in the virus' demands. The requirement of face masks made it mandatory for everyone to cover more than half of their face. And for those who disliked their face, they, for nearly two years, had the chance to go out in the world and not be ugly for once. Suddenly, while they were not beautiful, they were not hideous. Neutrality can do so much for someone. This period was like a gift for those with horrid teeth, large features, cystic acne, injuries, scarring, and discoloration. Never before were so many people looked straight in the eyes. Masks were some people's only chance to show who they were. And now, when the pandemic had ended, they were back in the shadows. Large groups of people, however, as Andrei had seen, still wore them, beneath the excuse that the virus could still return. *I would love to kiss one of you on the cheek*, he thought.

Andrei reached his home. He lived in a beautiful flat by himself—though it was more of a building that had offices than an apartment with proper tenants. The old, brick complex stood out among Gayley Avenue's modern real estate. It was a Jewish headquarters and temple that Andrei had asked to reside in due to its prime location. The stained-glass windows had caught his eye, so one day he walked in and they could not refuse his offer. The hotel job paid well— the liberal hourly wage, combined with the tips, combined with the company's ridiculous monthly appreciation raffles, made sure he was comfortable. He rented a large room and had furnished it with household collectibles and sculptures he'd found at estate sales. He'd installed a stove, renovated the restroom, and had a cleaning lady. Everything was in order. Though every time he returned home, calling out "Shabbat Shalom!" to the rabbis, he inserted his key and turned the silver knob and was faced with dread: what to do?

Freedom sounds phenomenal to the preoccupied young. But when one is an adult and has "free days" there is simply not much to do. Even in Los Angeles, where everything was. There was an unspoken spell of solitude cast on the city. Once one has been to the main parts of town, and had their fair share at the beach, Los Angeles turned unbreathably lonely. The biggest risks took place in grocery stores where a quiet shopper chose to switch to multi-grain bread after two years on sourdough. One could use their afternoons to create art—maybe writing a poem or painting a picture—all of which pass time but are isolating activities in and of themselves. The child begs for freedom and the adult wants to be told what to do.

It was also not so easy to make friends. Andrei had the option to remain friends with the boys he met in school, but came to realize they were not much of friends. He wanted to like them, love them even, but whenever he was in their company, he always checked his watch, tapped his foot, and searched incessantly for signals to leave. And at the end of the night, he would plop on his bed back home, drained, and hate himself for wasting his time on another false night. Friends, Andrei believed, were those unexplored newcomers we must want to know, rather than folks given to us and stuck with, but never had the courage to leave behind, or to consciously resolve on whether to keep them around. Andrei promised himself not to harbor near-friends, and instead, to develop truly until finding the humans exactly for him. In other words, he was nobly unhappy.

Andrei understood people were social animals who needed others to survive, but arguments that used biological outlines of life always creeped him out. He did not want to consider himself a thing that needed to gather in a group, or regard other evolutionary facts of his species, like needing to procreate or choosing a partner to make one feel safe. No. There were things he could choose between, like Earl Grey or jasmine green tea, children or no children, or having any friends at all.

Andrei avoided the internet as well and this evasion only added to his gloom. He loved music, especially old songs, and he loved movies, of all sorts. If he had the patience, sometimes he would read. While most of the pages he turned bored him to sleep, certain books with certain lines disarranged him. Some literature brought him to his feet, laughing and howling in his room. When the book was right, it was bliss and he wept. His room hushed with serenity and indebtedness. When he turned to his computer, however, or took out his phone, he would inevitably come across a viral trend or video that took the art he loved and turned it into a joke. The internet, in Andrei's desperate eyes, managed to make fun of everything serious. And if one did not laugh, they were not intelligent. The internet could not be slowed and no protest to criticize its exploitation of art could be made because recreations of art hid perfectly under the veneer of mockery and was thus, impenetrable. It was easy to use Chopin's 'Sonata No. 2' for a quick laugh, to reduce the 'Funeral March' to background music. It was a sneaky way for a digital creator to be considered an artist—and parodying the classics made them appear cleverer than the original artist. Meanwhile, Andrei's body had healed playing Chopin alone in his apartment. He would frailly replay movie moments, too, that he later found the world edited and ripped apart with its cheap teeth. And everyone ate the internet's crumbs. This cruel derision was impossible to escape. But enough jokes, memes, and glam over someone's precious source of life would eventually make a sensitive body numb. And Andrei was afraid of that. He needed his fountain of hope unblemished. For this reason, he escaped the internet's claws and only surrendered to it for e-mails, navigation, and the weather.

Andrei stared at his apartment door, unwilling to go inside this time. *There is nothing in there for me,* he thought. *Just some cloth and wood and aluminum.* And by some compulsion, he took the elevator down and began to circle the village, walking again, painfully, step by step.

Ahead of him, a couple laughed down the sidewalk. The blonde woman leaned her head on her man, brushing his arm.

"Look at him," Andrei thought. "He looks like one of those creepy production assistants who always happen to stand really close to a girl in yoga pants. Stubble. Plain-looking. 5'9" usually. Lazy, cynical. Not as soulful as the girl he ends up with. But it's the pervert they fall for. He criticizes things in his flat voice, but she will be drawn to that because it looks like carelessness and confidence. She'll find him mysterious because of a few dark interests that he has when, really, he is a pessimistic slob who is just fucked enough in his own head to ignore a woman and not scare her away with desperation the way normal men do."

But after all, the pretty girl is with him. Not Andrei, who felt like a negative number walking behind them. Then he thought, *There's no way I could.*

The girl turned her head around as her laughter finished and caught Andrei's shy eyes. She sent him a stony glare of polar dispassion. He felt a strange belonging to be in the hands of her unsympathetic expression. Andrei indulged in a pathetic helplessness and thought: "She's great. I'm dumb. How wonderful this placement is." He felt a sick, lovely comfort in their impossibility. It was something he could trust. He could slouch in the cold certainty of never getting close, never needing to hope, and never getting further than a look from afar or the graze of their shoulders. The girl grabbed her boyfriend's hands.

"Look at her," he said to himself. "Holding hands! She's probably already camped in the woods with him! Exchanged supernatural stories. Dinner dates. Shared food! Sex in the car! Concerts! I can never reach a woman like that. She's too experienced. What new could we do? Even if we were right for each other, I'd always feel small." Once lonely, it seemed the evolution of lonely was getting lonelier, as if sad heads boarded a lifeboat in an ocean that naturally pulled one farther and farther apart from the coast of love.

Andrei still hoped though. For that coast. That was the thing with this sailor—nothing was waiting for him, but maybe there was. Every time he met someone, his eyes were slightly far away, as if asking in his head: "It's nice to meet you, but are you there? Did you suffer and reach that place yet? You know that place. Those in that place know that place. After Tolstoy? After a thousand movies? Will you say an honest sentence?" Oh, did he beg, secretly, for strangers to meet him on that lonely floor of life—where life, still hard, was earned, and true, and golden. *The place*, he cried, *we recognize in media, binging in our beds, but don't dare reach on sidewalks.*

Andrei's feet wanted to move and his mind wanted to think. He set out to walk inside every major store in town.

That's what I'll do, he said to himself. He wondered if it was strange to stroll into shops with no interest to purchase anything. *God, I'm humiliating.* He felt vulnerable for wanting to meander and find something to do. *But maybe the actress at the hotel was right—humanity has done weirder things*, he thought.

He began at the farmer's market, since it was Thursday. It smelled of kettle corn and pupusas. Fresh produce was sold to young adults with backpacks and no bargaining skills. Other tents sold candles, crystals, croissants, and candy. Andrei observed young men his age, men on their way out of the planet, and men all the years in between.

The thing about guys his age, Andrei thought, was they all morphed into one big "bro." Certain phrases like, "Nah, you're good… damn, wow, that's sick… I appreciate you," have taken such enormous space in the air. Young men use them habitually, and accompany it with that general, polite airiness in the voice that communicates there is no incoming trouble. But that nice tone took a shape on vocal cords, and those phrases redesigned the brain all into one puzzle piece: the modern man. It was like taking a pair of scissors and cutting a man's unique shape into a rectangle, so all men could be properly put back into place, like gathering playing cards to be shuffled.

Often these rectangle men shrugged their shoulders toward the Air Force and wore green that did not match their crimson hearts. Or they considered digital ways to make money. Or forced their identities to seek refuge in a professional sports league. Some people may truly love entrepreneurship, their country, and Manchester United, but could all men? There was something suspicious to their alleged fascinations. *Do not at least three men here,* thought Andrei, *walking about this market, love the sun? So much that they want to camp and watch the plants grow? Anyone like to write little words on rocks and give them to people? Does anyone here who lifts weights love to lift people? Where is the flaming finger stretching out of the mold? They're all asleep!*

Andrei saw this male commonality most in fashion. He looked at the men with nicely fitted T-shirts and loose joggers. They all looked clean and what he knew convinced women would call "stylish." *Fashionable taste now means expensive clothing I guess*, thought Andrei. In one group, all the men wore costly hoodies— thick, simple, in a boxer cut, and colorful, so as to say, "This hoodie is orange because I have nothing to say—but that's okay because my hoodie is costly and my hoodie is orange." Or, "I've got rings on my fingers because it fills the space. And a cross that matches my outfit but carries a man I don't believe in." Not everyone needed taste, believed Andrei, but the trouble was giving it that name. *I can't say anything though. Even if it's true I'd sound like a prick. Believe that. How can we even—Christ! That's the problem with people living however they want. When anything goes, reason is no longer credible. You can't point out trouble. If the truth is offered, and they don't want it, they get to say the truth is a lie. Autonomy is now prioritized over understanding.*

Andrei closed his eyes and imagined his best outfit. *It would be a navy leather jacket and whatever pants and shoes. The jacket would do enough.* But he wore a costume the hotel gave him: a black silk shirt, beneath a lightweight, designer blazer, slim khaki slacks, and shiny brown Oxfords.

The hotel did not permit him to make many adjustments to the uniform, but he fought for a lengthy, gray summer scarf he spotted left behind in a suite a year back and added ever since.

Boredom still reigned over Andrei's day. So big a world, such little to do. He went over to a boba shop and ordered a large mango green tea with light ice, half sugar, and extra boba. Chewing on the tapioca pearls, he watched the world with a new filter. *Ah, life is sunny and fruity. I can be here longer.* But the 16 oz. trick only lasted ten minutes. Because boba only lasts for ten minutes. Because refreshments only refresh for so long. *Where do people find the happiness that lasts even after your final sip of a cold drink?*

Andrei did some more walking. *Damn, more walking!* he said to himself. There was a girl ahead of him, wearing a UCLA sweater, who he could not exactly catch up with. They walked at the same pace. He felt threatening being always exactly six feet away from her. He thought it would be sort of rude to walk past, so Andrei's legs lied to themselves and decided to walk slower than her. But then Andrei's rapid thoughts caused his feet to quicken, and he found himself closer to the girl. *Well, it's too late now,* he thought, and he picked up his speed and walked parallel to the college student. She glanced at him, a little alarmed. *Yup, I'm a creep.*

But a little light flickered inside him. Unsure of where it came from, or that it was even there, he wanted to try something. Andrei felt in his bones that a test was taking place: of who would not back down from this awkward staging. The spirited warrior would walk at his own pace, regardless of whether a civilian was shoulder to shoulder with him. *Let no other walkers influence your walk,* Andrei thought. And so for fifteen seconds, Andrei was the most courageous soul on Gayley Avenue and the young woman reading a book on her way to class was the most terrified.

He thought about doing more reading. It seemed the most comforting activity to do, except for one issue. Unlike a new movie, there was no one to immediately turn and talk to about a book. All books are strays. Books were read at the same time they were unknown at the same time they were revived at the same time they were forgotten. There was no agreed-upon trend of a novel. People found them on their own and all at different stages of life. This was why it was special to have the same favorite authors as a stranger, since both souls were in need of and privately searching for the same thing. A chapter could mean so much. But because Andrei could not share his excitement with anyone without misunderstanding or respectfully feigned interest, he ruled out reading as an activity. *And it takes too long to find someone who lived for the same page as you.*

4

THE CROSSWALK

Olivia grew up in a house in Malibu, where her parents sometimes lived too, and where the view was breathtaking.

She walked down Westwood Boulevard in brown boots, a black coat, and wore large silver headphones that played an Italian opera. Olivia did not understand the words of Luciano Pavarotti, but seemed to know why he sang and felt at peace every time she heard his tenor. To her, Pavarotti's voice was full of some untouched thing—an old island sunk too early to record or a child who has not discovered the meanness of the world. She spent so much time pretending, but listening to his voice shattered every possible illusion she could have of herself. If it were not for him, she would not be able to stand another day. She needed a source of goodness and it played at eighty-five decibels.

Olivia had to pretend. Life moved very fast to her. She was so often approached by men, who saw a full body that looked even better trying to hide. Boys in school said one thing to her, then another, and soon the wolves swayed the girl toward their dens. She had to pretend she was in control, that she had a choice, rather than reveal that ever since her body volumized, she had no idea what was going on or who she was. It was the curse of a body that grows faster than the girl inside it.

The girl attended a small high school near the coast, which was a crash course on drugs. Either the students sold substances or stole them from their parents to take themselves. To be fair, no one finds who they are in Malibu—the houses are too large. With high ceilings, so much to search and so little you, there was no reason to go inward. Once the friends come over, and the music plays, and the bag of ketamine spreads itself out on mother's granite kitchen table that was home to no cooking, there stood no chance for philosophy.

The day she graduated high school, and most of the men in her life had fled, Olivia locked herself in her room and threw up for days. Her life felt like a hobby others had attended to and abandoned. She was a pastime. A toy. And this disgusted her. She looked at her legs and all she saw was a rock climbing wall men had grabbed to launch themselves upward. She looked at her vagina and saw a slide that wanted to be out of order forever. Olivia was, to herself, a playground that never belonged to a single city or state, but one that merely came into the world and was tricked into thinking its purpose was to please her community. She always needed to prove herself—be more fun, sexy, and colorful. And when one or two men in her life looked at her, and dug their hands deep into her bark, she panicked, felt undeserving. She mistrusted those boys, rejected them, and sought out the nasty children who she could count on to vandalize her turf. Olivia was not just bad at love. She did not understand it.

In the years that followed, she found herself with attractive young men who did not hurt her. She felt secure with these boyfriends and Olivia was happy. But during a meal, inside the car, or in the early morning, these tall, harmless lovers did not seem to be made of anything. She looked closer. Olivia was in great company, a position many women would kill for, but her heart was never set ablaze. She could breathe and be herself, but in a way, she used them the same way she was once used: for a prerequisite purpose. She said to herself: "I love him. He doesn't bite. He is decent company." Most of those men simply woke up, ate, kissed her, talked about what the world talked about, and went to bed in the spacious apartment they shared. Her boyfriends did not care to notice Olivia retreating. They were simply content having a babe of a woman under their arm—but one day it scared Olivia when she realized that babe of a woman could have been any girl.

She did not confide or trust in these idle men. The men did not harbor secrets within their souls worth exchanging. They were athletic and pleased her physically every day, made a deal to feed her well, and kept a good-natured atmosphere, and this safety seemed like what love was supposed to amount to. But there was no darkness, and without darkness, there's no passion. And Olivia was right. Either the men broke their bond and cheated, or she did—and she would never again confuse satisfying times with beautiful men for love. To Olivia, love was reserved for… well, she did not know yet. She had not met him.

A small part of her despised romance. Men did such an unforgivable thing: they moved closer. Women were robbed of the experience to have a human man as a friend. Instead, he pretended, or manipulated her, and sadly ended up winning. And if he did not win, the friendship lost to restrained sentiments boiling under ordinary statements. The man was like some heartless stinger, headstrong to penetrate a relaxed orchid he promised to merely observe. But friendship with a man is what women, like Olivia, wanted the whole time. And she would never get it. Because of men. Because of women. Poor girl. And it did not help that women got so envious of each other, especially, for example, over Olivia's looks. She could feel their venom, if it was not directly spat at her, and found herself unable to withstand socializing with petty women who always gossiped about considerations she was naïve to and wanted to be naïve to!

What Olivia desired was someone to make her feel alive. She almost religiously drove out the dead past in her, practicing every day to recreate herself. Her most recent achievement was that she mastered the ability to see someone not for their appearance, but the spirit that comes out when they do or say something. This skill would flutter and certainly needed practice but when occurred felt sensational to her. A handsome man did not attract Olivia. There was no longer any value in the body to her. She knew skeletons as if raised in an oceanside cemetery.

Olivia did not pity herself. She was consuming Pavarotti, protecting her inspirations and sources of what life meant to her. Nothing obscene, false, or ugly tainted her days. This maintenance was an excruciatingly difficult exercise and all it looked like was a leisurely stroll.

A few feet ahead, Andrei walked on the same sidewalk, his face aimed at the ground like a seahorse. His eyes scanned the cement, which summed up love for him in a nutshell: common, dirty, and rough. What Andrei wanted was fair play. There were so many games to play when courting, like adding an air of mystery, keeping a distance, sending mixed signals, creating jealousy, and more, and so did not know for the life of him when he could release his heart.

Before, Andrei enjoyed letting his heart fly. He used to make breakfast in bed for his girlfriends, but it creeped them out. The boy was sweet in that he did not understand his acts were unordinary. He would insist on walking girls home and delighted in bringing them gifts he thought they would like, such as a piece of food or a flower. Andrei listened to women passionately. He agreed that while everyone picked a certain career in life, he favored to love. His singular wish for so long was to be a great husband, but none of his gestures were ever received with a proper welcome. Perhaps, he had no talent in this regard and was doomed to fail. Like Olivia, he tried to prove himself to his partners. Andrei planned creatively for anniversaries and simple dates, too, but they felt his scenes were unappealing and desperate, and they sometimes did not kiss Andrei or hold his hand. Their withdrawal left him unsure. Andrei soon felt ugly. When he looked in the mirror, he saw a horrible goblin out of place. When he held up his hand, it seemed scaly and misshapen. That was why he stared at the ground. When someone made eye contact, he believed he was being accused of something unpleasant. He could not accept there was any degree of handsomeness attached to him. He shied away from being received. *And how could I,* Andrei thought, *be received now, lowly as I am, if when I was animated and blessed with great energy and romance, was not even embraced then?*

Throughout the years, the ugly boy had lost belief in the practicality of love. He argued there would always be a better version of a man somewhere in the world and thus, no sound reason for a woman to commit to one. Plus, he believed, there was nothing to a woman—they did not love. They chose men for certain seasons and focused to enjoy life above all, in all its grandeur, intentionally saving sincerity for the end—once they were finished. How can men with eyes not sink into depression? And if a woman ever welcomed a man as a companion, she always smelled his feelings, which were gratifying and advantageous to her, and rosily sipped a man's glad spring of generosity until she was satiated. Andrei saw a woman's timeline and in response, froze his heart dry and hammered it to pieces. Steel or emptiness—these were the only two available armors available and adequate to withstand the ephemeral nature of women, who he regarded not as individual people, but as a collective entity of superficial vampires. So he promised himself he'd never woo the dead.

But some nights, when he listened to a folk song, sung by a woman strumming a ukulele, his chest roasted. The female sings in softness gentle lyrics that stake his cold heart and light a tiny campfire right on the surface. "Maybe," his flames say, "we want to be shaken and loved enormously."

The singers Andrei listened to seemed to want something whole, like him. It may be that he needed a friend. A good friend, perhaps a female who did not feel like an adversary, but a rescuer who, too, needed rescuing. But right then, Andrei scanned the sidewalk and did not look up.

Andrei noticed some stranger's nice brown boots to the left but thought nothing of it. Olivia felt a slow shadow on her right and heard Pavarotti's cries. And the two puzzle pieces of people continued, not seeing each other, and never would, and within a few steps of their own, walked perfectly past.

5
THE HARDWARE STORE

Andrei sometimes wondered how much a river would change Los Angeles.

He pictured a long stream of water that divided the city, much like the River Thames or the Seine. Rivers nourished. The water happily rewrote the aisles of streetlamps and transformed one's nighttime walk into a feature film. It carried boats filled with a surveying crowd that waved back at any brandishing hand on land that tried. It fostered lunch dates, amusing dares, and a reference for the lost.

Andrei had spent one summer abroad and met these rivers. He was astonished at the difference in conversations the Europeans had with him. They were simple and alive. The pubs helped. The accents, too. *Was it the rain that reminded?* he speculated. *The museums? The red buses? The cheap flights to any neighboring country? So—what was it about the geography of LA that made connection impossible?* Just then, the sun glared at him. He glared back.

Once that triumphant sun gloated, Andrei blinked back to the street. He eyed a young lady with short, dark hair who waited at the other end of the crosswalk. She wore a tight red

A HAPPY GHOST

sweater that Andrei eyed first. Humans—it meant something when a woman wears red. They locked eyes for one second and their lives were the other's, as vision makes it so, until a passing car blocked them both and the two looked away, at some general else. Eleven seconds displayed on the opposing cross signal until the two young souls would meet each other. But Andrei wanted more than a crossing. He wanted some fire, a clash, a collision of some sort.

When it was time to walk, his mind searched for a rope to pull a conversation out of the short-haired girl. Then her grocery bag ripped open and fresh produce spilled on the street.

Andrei crossed over to her, running, and realizing his questionable speed, slowed down.

"Oh, I got you," he said.

"No, it's okay!" said the girl.

No, it's okay? he thought. *Well, folks, she rejected my help, so she does not like me at all and therefore there is no future for us whatsoever in any chance in any world—* but actually, the girl wanted his help and was not quite sure why the first thing she told this boy was "no."

Andrei picked up her groceries and struck up a conversation.

"I usually ask if they can double bag them," said Andrei.

"Oh, really?" she let him go on.

"Yeah, for safety and all."

She smiled as Andrei continued to recover her groceries.

"Well, now you know what I eat," said the girl.

"Ah yes... paper towels and... dish soap!" said Andrei.

"Yes, exactly!"

He eyed her fingernails, painted bright blue. Her wrists smelled like peppermint and she said her name was "Stella." Andrei was impressed by her femininity, the subject of which was a dangerous thing. When some men are exposed to a certain kind of woman, they become so absolutely entranced by their iridescence that they would do anything to be around them for longer. Lie. Linger. Kill. It was a pure, wild attraction, that started from a collarbone, that would make a man agree to rip out his tooth if only to hear a woman talk again. Lastly, she had these devilish eyes exclusive to brown and only ever sometimes encountered. Those types of eyes were so dark they had death in them, but were framed with such sweet, narrow eyelids that took death, swirled it in a sizzling adorableness, and communicated a dangerous, impatient capability for sex. It seduced men throughout history—what lived behind the mischievous, delicate, hickory fire.

They moved to the streetlight and Stella carried her bag with crossed arms. Andrei briefly wondered where those eyes would take him, except a boy never really understands a girl. He just sort of keeps guessing. She was fond of Andrei's company and he of hers, but he broke eye contact and made a choice to come to a halt. Their mutual enjoyment stayed right where it was.

Sometimes, flirtation that led to nothing was everything. The coquetry remained harmless. If fortunately ceased, momentary sparks would not be damaged by a chair-throwing, divorce-filing, property-debating future. It was one of life's little treats to meet someone amazing, have perfect chemistry, and walk away flattered and regretful, and best of all, forever remember a stranger who was so right and yet, by then, so far away. A perfect memory tastes sweeter than an exhausting series of normal ones. People could have each other without possession. Nothing needed to last forever when good memories lasted forever.

I don't want to spoil us with the color red, he thought.

The young lady sensed Andrei had come to an agreement on where things would go.

"Well, it was nice to meet you. Thanks for your help," she said.

"Goodbye." Andrei waved. He watched her walk off with the ripped bag held cautiously in her arms as the bells of the Catholic church on Hilgard Avenue chimed.

A new hour.

His generation was uncertain if God existed. Having had parents who were religious and breaking off from them, they had associated childhood apathy with religion. But larger than that, this generation was unsure why human life existed—and no matter what technology was invented, there was, in everyone, an incontestable hole. But the internet came, with its limitless span, and for the first time, something was vast enough to challenge that hole. To challenge God. The world needn't question the universe when it was in the palm of their little hands.

Andrei entered a hardware store.

It was a panorama of flashing monitors, speakers, computers, cellphones, repair booths, and appliances. None of which would fully exist without the global system of interconnected networks that was the internet.

The effects of the internet could best be summed up by man's failed capacity to understand it in time. It had burst into their species like a bomb and pulled its users so far apart from each other. An updated stream of videos, links, comments, porn, online shopping, games, news, and socials gave no air for people to slow down and gather themselves. Hope for recollection was lost. No glue could repair the devastation of a splintered race. It was over. There were so few studies on this phenomenon that the public regarded, largely because no one could comprehend the enormity of such a dangerous invention, that was if researchers were not distracted by it themselves. The internet was also a tool that changed what man needed to know, in terms of selecting what information was worth brain space over a quick mobile search for an answer. A tool that changed how people read each other—no longer discerning micro body language in interactions, but pre-measuring a person with infographics and stylized images. A tool that would always be referred to as a tool, protected by its aptitude that forever voided it of being successfully accused of its unintended, genocidal function.

Down the aisle from Andrei, a woman, mid-thirties, scanned the collectibles shelf. There hung bobbleheads, keychains, and fan gear of popular television shows. The lady stood in her black puffer jacket. On the back, it read: "San Francisco." She wore it hooded. The lady had a flat nose and pretty eyes where the Bay's thick fog still flowed steady. If she spoke, it was relaxed, and her breaths were synchronized to the tranquil rocking motion of present ships at Fisherman's Wharf. She was a city girl, which hardened her, and she smelled like fresh cannabis. Her glamorous, narrow fingers were shaking. Even as she held a bobblehead in her hand, Andrei thought: *Is she hungry? Is she afraid? Are her rings too heavy?* Spying, Andrei caught that the tchotchkes she shopped for were all in the cartoon genre.

Live-action television, with actors, didn't interest her. She preferred watching adult animals argue, or some absurdist space animation that made her laugh after work. It was a cozy world she could trust. Shows with real faces disappointed her. Maybe she did not believe the performance. Maybe it was another cameraman showing off. Maybe, most likely, it was that this woman was at a time in her life where she was exhausted by people, even hated them, and hated their lies, and merely looking at another person's fictional crime broke her heart. She still craved connection, but animation provided her with life without the living. Should she explain her interest to anyone wondering, the idea would struggle to transfer. She would go back to the curious interviewer one week later and say: "Actually, I was wrong. I don't prefer cartoons because the stories are more interesting... I just don't like seeing real people all the time... Or it's not that exactly. I hate people. No, that's not true... sorry, let me think about it." But there was no further thinking to be done. She understood it. And her intention remained within her until one day she confessed to a co-worker:

"I prefer cartoons because they don't remind me of anything, but make perfect sense," she said.

And her co-worker stood still. A tingling emotion arose in them so complex and sad that it served as one of those pure thoughts one remembered sometime in their day, recurring, over many years, possibly until the end of time, when they were silent and recalling the handful of things they had encountered which were real. Sometimes these treasures were sentences, maybe looks a person had given them, or in this instance, the feeling of understanding a woman's older need for cartoon television shows.

When the San Francisco woman left, Andrei stood in her spot, took the same product she'd carted, and bought it. It was a toy mermaid who smiled and held a bottle of rosé. He exited the store and tucked the collectible inside his blazer pocket.

The revving of an obnoxious motorcyclist rang in his ears as it zoomed past. He loved motorcycles—the smell of gasoline and its rugged spirit of freedom—but hated the damn noise.

Andrei rode one himself most days. If his bicycle could not do the job, he took his old 2005 Triumph Street Scrambler he bought used on Craigslist. He loved his bike for the same reason he loved the rain: its reminder that life, in an instant, could be otherwise. The choice to purchase a bike was not impulsive, but it was quick.

To Andrei, it was so clear that a motorcycle was in his future. The afternoon he'd seriously considered it was the afternoon he'd purchased one. He'd wanted a motorcycle since he was a child, but Andrei's parents had never allowed him to ride a "death machine." He recalled his mother, one day, at a museum. A 1941 Norton 16H in military green modeled in one of the exhibits. Andrei was a young boy and his mother encouraged him to mount it.

"Go, go!" she called happily. And she took a photo of Andrei, seated right there, with his tiny hands on the enormous handlebars and she said, looking at him: "You look so handsome, my love."

She loved Andrei on a motorcycle, but if she were to know he rode one, the last thing she would snap was a photo of him. She would order him to sell the bike, give up the plates to the DMV, and cut up his motorcycle license, even though Andrei was truly meant to be seated on a two-wheeler. A phenomenon occurred where his mother's love for him got in the way of loving *him*. It was like preventing a musician from going on tour because one would miss them for so long: the person they claimed to miss was in fact the soul that belonged on stage and never to them. Love for a person was accepting they kill themselves the way they want to be killed. His mother was a case of possession triumphing identity. As Andrei changed, her love did not follow him, the way affection must trace the renewal of its subjects, but remained still and stale and otherwise, false. She had many photos of her son but in this way did not know what he actually looked like.

Aside from his instinctive attraction to bikes, Andrei had learned why he rode as his mileage grew. The first reason Andrei rode was his moonlight reason. When he rode at night, to side streets that heard no voice, and affluent neighborhoods that inhabited no walkers, he acknowledged the part of him that rode a motorcycle for love. His 2005 Triumph made him want to meet a very special girl. One day, he would inevitably crash and be thrown off his bike and he would see for one second during that fatal toss, a final face remembered airborne. She may or may not have existed as a person. He imagined her eyes would collect every eye color from every woman he had ever met. And before imagining that final face, he had to find her somehow. But if he failed to, that was okay. He rode to die and would die to meet a mythical woman he would never know. No one was exempt from wanting final faces.

The second reason was that the exposure to danger gave him an unnatural calmness in the real world. Not everyone was voluntarily exposed to a high likelihood of gruesome death shortly after having brushed their teeth, and to mount on a bike was to accept that one could turn into a gravestone in the blink of an eye any ordinary morning.

This drama made up a large part of who he was. He chose things. He left when something did not suit him. He was in control when pressured. This special fervor cut through many inconsequential things—shaving off frivolous matters, but leading him to boredom faster.

There was also a term for bikers called "target fixation." When a rider looked at something for too long and focused on a passing object, or any small distraction to the left or right of him, he had an increased chance of colliding with that object. It was extremely dangerous to fixate. Any concentration expended that was not ahead of the rider oftentimes resulted in severe injury or death. A biker who wanted to live must not be thrown off course. And after miles and miles of riding, of looking ahead, of sixty mile per hour winds piercing his neck, the gloss of his eyes hardening, he naturally never target fixated on things or people either.

It was hard to invest in a person when one saw how things passed. Take the ball player, for example, who dedicates his life, gets injured, and then watches the sport proceed without him. He sits on his leather couch, watching better athletes run across his television screen, younger ones on renovated fields. And he, who sacrificed his sweat, youth, and sanity to the sport and knew coaches, teammates, and even janitors at the stadium like brothers—is forced to still live afterward. His teammates said kind words before a match, hugged him after a goal, but now seem to be focused on new seasons and new goals. He gets left behind. Did none of it mean anything? He cries for the fast world to stop and says, "Slow down. This pains me. We were just here. I used to joke with you. We said we loved each other. Wait for me. Will you just wait for me?" Those hands he shook after a victory could not care for the weeping, broken-footed man hiding in the shadows of his home, once lit by the sun, once the life of the party.

k.f.

When Andrei walked into a job now, or even met someone for the first time, he thought: *How long will it take you to forget me?*

6

THE CAFÉ

Andrei walked inside a vibrant café in Westwood. The place was floored in checkered marble: salmon and white. There were a dozen mosaic tables and the bathroom, a reliable indicator of the quality of a merchant's product, was spotless. Behind the front glass window, a flashy green curtain hung from the ceiling. The shop was buzzing.

On his way in, Andrei ran into a familiar face. David was his name. David waved and smiled. He exuded such overwhelming energy to the target-fixated Andrei that Andrei wanted to grab a pump, remove all the air from David's head, and then say: "Can you just talk to me normal, mate?"

David was Andrei's old co-worker at the hotel, with whom Andrei could never quite ease into. He had no reason to mistrust David—the man was not cruel or deceptive. But there was a certain type of social person who says all the right things but is just so acutely off. There is a slight craze in their vitality. Something rehearsed about their behavior. Either their eyes are open wider than normal or they do not blink as often. They smile but at the same time look like they are going to turn their necks three hundred and sixty degrees and scream out into the sky, in shame they have betrayed themselves.

David always repeated motivational sentiments and hid behind the modern lifestyle of hustle and productivity. David would ask how Andrei was doing, but one sensed it was not because he cared, but because he wanted to compare Andrei's days with his own. *But David will change,* thought Andrei. *This lie of his may last long, but not forever.*

"People need to meet more people because when people meet people, people see themselves in people and over time, try to become less like the people they dislike and more like those they do," said Andrei to himself.

It was difficult to point these folks out, to put them on trial. How could one dislike a nice person? They said all the right things. Some people like David even went to the extent of being self-deprecating. It was a strategy of invulnerability. For example, they might apologetically acknowledge they were "talking too much" or sprinkle phrases like "Ah! I'm so self-absorbed" so as to exclude themselves from any claim of narcissism. Or when they achieved things, they perfectly said they were grateful and honored. Though at home, they hungrily harbored self-interest and greed. People praised their humility and, lacking the patience to notice that tiny bullseye of falseness, called those people humble. All it took for the humble people to be humble was to break the fourth wall of ego. To announce there was a snake in the room allowed them to never be suspected of being a serpent. No one saw the serpent. But one detected when it was there. It bothered a listener quietly. Some blockade prevented Andrei's soul from resting.

"It's so good to see you! I hope you're doing well!" said David, as if conversations were e-mails.

"How are you, David?"

"Blessed man, can't complain. Did you hear?" asked David excitedly.

"Hear what?"

David milked a few seconds of Andrei's attention and relished in the power of knowing an unknown thing. Andrei wondered why the pause. Then David announced in a voice of after-shock the news that a celebrity had overdosed in their bathtub that morning. From the contrived suspense, Andrei got a dirty feeling from the guy—as if the terrible death of a person did not actually matter to David. It just gave David something to say.

"It's crazy, man. He was so young too."

"Yeah."

Ah, that's why, Andrei thought. This type of breaking news had a particular effect, an effect listeners can only react one way to, that its messenger gets to inspire, wear the captain hat as they deliver the blow, and seem mighty, even sympathetic.

"It's terrible. Anyway, let's get lunch soon," called David. Andrei simply smiled, hated that even. *He took a smile from me,* he thought sadly. He wished to tell David that he'd rather not, but hesitated and let him go.

Lunch, yes. It was always lunch. But oh, how much money and time would be saved if two people agreed to a bench, faced each other, and said what they wanted.

Andrei ordered with the cashier. He looked at her closely. She was not as pretty as he had liked. But he studied her and adjusted his attraction, trying to find something—the way, for example, a lonely observer might have done at work when they wished their colleague to be beautiful since no one else around was, nor their town, and so settled for the illusion. People readjusted beauty all the time. When discouraged enough, a hoping individual could look at a person while the brain made re-calculations, subtracting the other person's ugliness, imagining their features as "a little less that" and a "little more this." And within a few seconds, the ugly became the needed pretty.

"I love the curtains in the front. The green," he told the cashier.

"Oh… Me too—they're—my favorite part about this place," she said.

He was intrigued by how the cashier operated at her own tempo. She talked slower than he expected, as if there were extra spaces between her words, and would look fixedly at a point in the room for longer than anticipated with slightly droopy eyelids. Andrei even guessed the woman had mild autism. She had long, red hair that he liked—and moved her body unpredictably, turning one way sharply. She would also not react to expressions he made that would usually prompt a reaction in most people. Before she responded, she held his sentence in her eyes and for a second nothing moved and the air was awkward. Andrei knew three types of pauses in conversation. The first was respectful and made normally, usually to allow a speaker to complete their thought. The second type of pause is so long that two people have to acknowledge it, either with a laugh or a question relating to the pause. The third type of pause is encountered in certain public areas and is gradually, almost guiltily, identified as a trait from the person they are talking to and so must quickly go along with in a behaved performance before one risks offending them. She paused like the third and spoke as if reading familiar lines from a book. He felt ashamed that he was attracted to her neurodivergence. There was something honest about it, and he felt very strong around her, wanting to, for no reason except his body's declaration—dominate. It was very strange, so he quickly paid for his drink and left.

The café was decorated with pink walls matching the floor. Hung around the space were old mirrors, glass cases with miscellaneous vintage objects, like broken camera lenses, corks, and an array of different-sized lightbulbs. It housed bamboo-laced chairs, resembling those of a Paris streetside. The room played the music of conversation—for instance, a couple whispering to each other, an old man laughing on his phone, and the 1-1-2-1 finger tapping of a student with their classmates as they experienced a silent moment in their dialogue.

It was amazing how simple all these sipping persons appeared compared to the quiet disaster in their minds. Shall we look?

Stephanie had graduated from university six years ago. She remembered her past as she gazed at the young girl across the room who looked almost like her. *Look at her,* she thought. Stephanie recalled moments in lecture when she had been her age and impressed the room with her response. Another memory that arose were the phone calls she would get of her family members passing on, as college usually marked the time when little girls lost their grandparents. Nostalgia and death swirled around her head, like the froth above her latte. She cupped the mug; it was warm in her hands.

Stephanie's main problem was that her thoughts cycled. The same sorrows and the same hopes were intertwined in her head, seven days a week, never introduced to another path of light. "I can feel my body getting old... I want to run my own company... I wish I could re-live college... I can feel my body getting old... I want to run my own company...I wish I could re-live college..." she repeated. She wanted to break that cycle. Stephanie desired to start her human all over again—but the tattoos on her fingers, arm, and leg kept her stuck in the same year she'd felt she needed them. It was hard to think of life outside her shell when it was painted permanently with old ideas. She was actually healthy. It was the ink that weighed. She even had a fresh smiley stamp on her hand from a music festival. If Stephanie woke up and wanted to fight her tattoos, she would lose. It was too fun being entertained on the weekends so she let herself be tranquilized by entertainment.

Earlier, what seemed like yesterday, while she was attending school, she was cushioned. Then parking tickets, taxes, and the chaos of a world that minds its own completely shocked the student. She wanted to curl up in a ball on fluffy bedsheets and waste a day without feeling left behind. A cleanse of some kind would be nice for her. Stephanie needed to escape the body that comfortably sheltered her pain.

Her true skin color was a light beige, like the skin of pencil shavings, and was soft as it was when her mother lotioned her before bed every night. Stephanie did not have the memory of those nights, but they were the reason she subconsciously pumped two servings of shea butter before she sleeps. Mothers lived in a child forever, the way their own mothers lived in them. With one mother's kiss, a child received a recipe made by a thousand seasoned souls—a generation of love transferred in everything a woman did. Stephanie sipped her coffee and searched for a way out.

Beside Stephanie, a date took place between Elijah and Lyn. Elijah was a handsome, stocky man with a curly beard and tired, childish eyes that fought to see the good. Lyn wore teashade prescription glasses, which complimented her sharp features. Always calm, she had an oval face, full lips, and still working on her immaculate teeth, wore retainers, which was heard in her speech and gave her ravishing looks an accessible, geeky charm.

Elijah slid forward an empty piece of paper.

"I'd like you to write to me."

"Write to you?"

He nodded.

Her look, light and testing, asked him why.

"You're unbearably beautiful. Yeah, yeah, yuck. You know that, whatever. But you're pretty, which is concerning, for me. Because, well, I need to know your thoughts and understand you. I'm afraid to mistake the impression of your beauty for, you know…"

"Love," she said, boldly.

"Love," he said. "Yes, love," he repeated. "I want you to tell me something, anything. But a lot of it. I don't think we're how we look like. I want to know the voice on that paper." He pointed and offered her a pen.

Lyn began to write.

The contents of her letter would serve as the seed for Elijah's love. He chose to love her in a form that was concentrated and undistracted, which she valued and had never considered herself. She asked he write to her as well—and from then, they would exchange theories, sentiments, and secrets, and their love was as pure as the green Sencha that steamed dewily on their table.

Beside them sat a man in his late forties who burned his tongue on a cinnamon coffee. The instant it stung, he recalled his frustration with past partners; it was that neural connection between pain and the bedroom. He recently found that sex was sex, and it was disappointingly unidimensional. It was rubbing skin. Nothing more. And he'd had plenty of fun as a city man already. *Some people*, Edgar thought, *prefer strong foods, like the overwhelming taste of chocolate—but some appreciate more delicate flavors like pumpkin spice, sesame, orange peel, pickled lotus, or lavender. Chocolate is certain, but does vanilla on the other hand not arouse the mind, saying, "Oh, wait a moment, is it this or… let's give it another lick?"* He figured there were less obvious pleasures to indulge in: indulgences that increased one's spectrum of preference. That was what Edgar thought of things. And in the case of sex with others, there were more enjoyable activities in life to him—such as attending a play, napping in gardens, or dressing up nicely on a day where you entirely stayed at home. He'd spent far too much time chasing the large and immediate hole of ecstasy when there were other amusements to attend to. *But sex isn't all bad,* Edgar countered. And he recalled a memory or two. When sex had nuance, such as the last time he would meet a person, or when he hated another so much he must have them another way, when it *meant* something—Edgar believed those engagements "no longer turn us into mere animals, but humans." Edgar debated within himself which sex was worth more: incredible and energetic, or curiously complicated to the point of sorrow? He sensed that the light of life, with his lowered eyes that had done too much, strangely only flickered back up again during the latter.

Beside him was a small employee sweeping the floor, just by Andrei. The cleaner clenched the broom with effort and quick movements. She moved forcefully, with so much vigor that one saw a girl scout. But wrinkles had already formed on her neck, that sweated, moistening her black wig. Andrei stared, noticing she was damn good at her job, but too good. She would bend her legs to sweep the difficult corners of the shop. The woman would adjust the picture frames on the wall and wipe down the chairs, tasks which were not part of her required duties. Whenever her co-workers talked casually, the woman steered the conversation to the topic of the conditions of the store, which she knew, or to certain customers, who she knew, or to how business was, which she knew. She drove back home with a smile, knowing she'd done a great job that day. "They need me! Otherwise, who else would have caught the slip hazard by the trash? No one, not even my manager!" she would say before bed. She was naturally helpful. It was tragic to see that kind employee, happy like a little child, be so great at some stupid shop, when in her pumped a heart large enough to fuel the future, a forest, or a country. There was no structure of life, or invention yet created, whose mechanism could righteously allocate the innocence and love embedded in the warm blood of a human being. There deserved to be. She was sacred. But the world, decidedly corporate, had seized her, eaten her up, devouring what was left of the lively.

Andrei could not bear her smile in the context of their atmosphere. The worst part was when her manager thanked her, she bowed her head and clasped her accomplished palms together, feeling truly recognized. She walked away, hands gripped behind her back, shoulders back, neck like an arrogant bird and gait like a soldier, searching the unworthy ground for a spot of dirt.

"What is this place really?" Andrei said to himself.

The line moved one order at a time. The staff in the back labored with commotion. Andrei looked out the front window and saw a car scoping out a parking spot. And as his mind zoomed out, Andrei saw the shop as a method created by an intelligent species to distribute nutrition for their hungry, animal stomachs. It was a nice development—to mold a large box of plaster and drywall, paint it nicely, and dedicate it for merchandise. It was quite dull and exhausting most of the time: the impatient line shuffled, the room buzzed, the blender was too loud, the AC stopped, and those on a date entered inside and worried who was to pay for what. Still, all the hearts beat in the room the same way they did next door or a century ago in a ballroom in Versailles. This beating would never change, regardless of how much the rooms did. The sight of humans around each other was enough to hang around until closing.

Another date occurred, over by the corner. A young man in maroon politely giggled as he and his partner talked about all the shows they were watching.

"Jean, that was so good, right? And did you watch the spin-off?" he asked.

"No! I haven't," she said.

"Also, very good."

"You know what was great was… Yes! It was the main actress who's in that old show," she offered.

"Prince of T?"

"Prince of T! Yes. Highly recommend."

The unfortunate reality of modern conversations was they consisted of recommending the endless sea of film and television media. And by mentioning all the content one consumed, the two could never dive deep into one, and instead ping-ponged their way to recommend more until suddenly the date was over and there was nothing to remember having learned about the other person.

Jean took a bite of her pastry and the man in maroon took private pleasure in watching her eat. He loved watching the creature chew the food he picked out for her, munching it like a rabbit that has no awareness of its charm. He enjoyed seeing her swallow it, the way a busy child so naturally consumes a box of apple juice, and then lastly, watch her lips stretch to confirm tasty nourishment. The man in maroon wished for all the nutrients to reach her body, distribute equally and timely, so that even if the date did not go any further, his meek existence at least contributed to her beauty with a single, pathetic guava strudel.

"I actually traveled to Spain and saw where they filmed."

"No way!" he said.

"Yeah, last year! I spent the whole summer there and met literally the best people. It's so beautiful there." Jean smiled.

"Tell me more," he said.

"Spain—well, you wake up every day so energized. I miss a lot of the friends I made—we'd just go out dancing every night and have the best lunches and get drinks in the most amazing places. Have you been?"

"Once, but I was a little kid," he said to Jean with a small laugh. She nodded and sipped her coffee, and he did the same, but the hot latte tasted cold. It was something that he said which for some reason slowed his heart. He loved hearing Jean talk about Spain, but felt himself shrinking in his chair and turning into a little bug.

"I'd kill to go back," said Jean.

Jean continued on and the moment was impossible for him. *The bars she partied in Barcelona were way better than the shop we're in now,* he said to himself. His heart plummeted further down. *She always brings up these stories that are far more interesting than when we meet. How she took ecstasy and went to afterparties—that never happens when we're together. Do I hold her back? Does she deserve better?* His face lied and he did his best to respond with enthusiasm, but he felt his body turn into goo. One ought not to tell others of their dear travels. The past was better and was extremely competitive. Jean's date felt that he could not offer the same quality of life she had experienced in Spain. He could not be her new Spain. Because Spain was mentioned.

Jean let her private mind float a little longer, remembering the music she'd heard and men that had held her in Barcelona. But she wished that she had remained quiet and not talked about her summer. There was a reason she returned to LA.

Jean checked her watch and was about to say she better get going. Jean would say it with the shaky voice he'd noticed come out. And throughout their date, there had been periods of oddness from her that did not fit the moment. To mask her nerves, the girl would utter bold and cold sentences. Her face would mutate to a neutral slate, as cool as the figure in a portrait painting, when they were actually talking about something lovely. She had not noticed this habit herself, but her date was taken aback by this characteristic and spent much time trying to recover from the pauses. *What's the issue?* he thought.

The moment was slipping, and the young man in maroon could not take another loss. He asked Jean:

"Why is it awkward with you?"

She looked at him.

"Not in a bad way," he added quickly, in order to give her some kind of conversational rope to tease him back with, which she caught:

"Bad way?" she replied.

"Yeah. Are you, like, nervous?" he said. He did not understand her. What he really wanted to ask Jean was: "Have enough people told you that you're great?" He saw her character as so fragile and awkward that she might be one of those people who was indeed alluring, but who went about this world generally uninformed of their better qualities. Perhaps some passersby had never delivered Jean compliments, either on her personality or appearance. Maybe they were too occupied with admiring her, too timid to share the news, or most of the time, mistaken in thinking she already knew.

She did not know. The boy in maroon was right. Not many people had told Jean she was pretty. She had a kind of look about her that others always wondered: "Who is she and what is she going to do next?" Obvious beauties were complimented within seconds. Hers was a captivation that loosened jaws. And from the world's silence, she felt unattractive, unworthy, less than a normal person.

"Just tired," she said.

"Okay. Do you know that you're... I think you're... yeah, my bad."

And they left it at that.

A woman across typed at her pink laptop until she sipped on her mocha. It was expensive to find the right place to do work. She tried one café and then another, but this week, she might have finally found a place that fit. She liked loud rooms. Quiet ones made her uneasy. It was as if twenty normal persons created enough energy for the lively one she was. Ashu was her name. She wore a brown hijab and journaled about where she went—because she was missing. Ashu was once so animated and hilarious. Ashu would jump in the air mid-conversation, wave her hands, tease others, face the ceiling to laugh sweetly in contralto, and dance out her sentences—all of which seemed out of place in writing, but were impulses that made sense in her conversations. Except the world had judged her soul with their dull hearts. Her family. Co-workers. Female friends. Ones she gave her gestures to. They made Ashu feel like a freak. Her boss at her workplace once even told her to tone it down.

"Tone what down?" she asked, with a confused smile.

"Everything."

She agreed and began to doubt herself. Maybe she was a bit excessive after all. And perhaps, thought Ashu, her way of having fun was unprofessional. And so she turned her origami inside out and became as square as them. The best part of Ashu was killed. In actuality, everyone who accused her of being too large secretly marveled at Ashu's largeness. It was the best thing about their day! It was why they smiled on their drives back home, went to work excited to talk to her, and even adopted some of her mannerisms. But when standing before Ashu, those people did not know how to react to her and met her instead with disapproval and confusion. Anytime they sensed her grandness could be called overdone, and felt a need to assert grandness for action's sake, they pulled her aside to give her some life advice on serenity. They intervened not because they were truly bothered, but because it gave them something to notice, to correct, and thought they were helping her. Ashu did not want to be helped. She wanted to live. *Where have I gone?* she typed in her laptop diary. *Why did I let them take me?*

A man shined to her left. He was called Lorenzo and he drank a hot chocolate with whole milk. He sipped it with fleshy, pink lips and gulped it down his large neck that seemed to be a kind of engine. The gulp went down his chest, where his muscles cooled after his calisthenics, and sunk somewhere behind the walls of his tight, tan stomach. He was a chess set of a man. He had burly knights as biceps, thick bishops as legs, healthy pawns as his troop of fingers, and the battlement of rooks as his fortified abs of stone. Lorenzo was charismatic and handsome. Despite his loud body, he was soft-spoken and whispered as he talked. And not a raspy, deep whisper, but a light decency that sounded like song. His eyes were dark cacao and blinked in such a way one could tell he was a momma's boy. He was at the café to clear his mind. Lorenzo interned at a local theatre, shadowing a prominent sound designer. An upcoming show was nearby and he was tasked with operating the soundboard for the first half.

Lorenzo was nervous and needed to run through some cues. That tiny sheet of paper in his large hands might have seemed strange to someone who acknowledged his bulging veins. "Why is he not holding metal? Why is he behind the scenes and not on stage? He should be photographed!" But he did not mind. Lorenzo was perfectly at peace. Beautiful people were led to think their beauty needed to go somewhere. On a person's phone. In a magazine. Outwards. Why do anything with it? Maybe all the models on runways loved it, but maybe most just walked in because they fit inside the doors. Here was a pretty man who did not share himself and very much could have. It was rare to meet someone with that kind of jaw, sweet eyes, and those arms, who did not fall into modeling or influencing. There was magic in this. Lorenzo inadvertently alchemized his reserve into a valuable currency: the only time someone could see his beauty was if they were in the same room he was in or if they heard about it from someone who *was* there. Lorenzo had planted a kind of beauty in the world not captured by a camera, but a beauty that passed through and could only ever be run into.

And lastly were his irises. He had no social media, which quieted and calmed his gaze, and freed his eyes of self-satisfaction. Contemporary eyes looked at their own photos for so long a time that they concocted a double version of themselves—some internet shadow manifesting itself in controlled movements aimed to replicate the self they assessed as the sexiest. Lorenzo was simply a man who lived meal to meal, saw friends, and let go of his face.

Beside him was Amanda, who felt such relief from sitting. She stood all day. Her prolonged uprightness, being a waitress, caused blood to flow to her feet and calves, and inflamed her lower body. But this physical consequence of serving was not the actual pain she suffered.

Amanda felt out of sorts. When she waited tables, especially working at an upscale steakhouse a block away, it was her job to satisfy. She needed to make a tip and amplify parts of herself that appealed to customers. She laughed, listened, joked, recommended, and responded—quite well—all day putting on a kind of front. She was in control of this part of her job. With men, she knew their weak points, targeted them, and it worked like a spell. Although a little insecure about her ears, she was aware of her good looks. Amanda understood which words worked best, the angles to serve a plate, and when to stroke a person's ego. But her control of the cards was, after all, an illusion. Amanda might have known the tricks, but this did not change the prescribed dynamic of obedience. The customers held the strings. She worked to falsify her movements, adjust her timings, and say sentences with no will. Amanda could not manage what only a few months of this did to her. In a way, though all she did was converse and serve meals, when she put up her apron and sat still in her car, her day job felt to her like sex work. She hated that hollow, end-of-the-day exhaustion of being a puppet.

Table by table, Amanda would lose parts of herself, those parts being snatched unforgivingly by hungry strangers who paid for them. They paid for her to stay longer. They paid for her will to say, "Back off." They paid for her to come back and ask them about how their workdays were. She felt fractured in a job that appeared usual and common. But in actuality, serving went beyond a stressful shift. When Amanda sold herself over sixty times an afternoon, she reached a soul-destroying state. One could only play a character for so long until there was no one to return to.

Amanda recovered in her alone time. Off the clock, she did not want to be pulled. This was why she was such a private person.

The waitress discovered treasure in privacy. Amanda could not bear telling her friends everything she knew or did. Once she did, life became a system of relaying events to people and keeping that roster of listeners current with new, worthless updates.

And she did not want to be consumed. She even sensed a hesitation to tell others what book was in her bag after she felt that the intimacy between her and the author was somehow lost when shared. Amanda understood that people were not what they exuded, but what they held. She was to accumulate herself. *Do not spill,* she repeated to herself. It was a skill to keep one's conflicts inside. It was so easy to pull another person in and spread one's mess.

Normally, people felt better after releasing their problems, though this infuriated Amanda. She worsened afterward for a number of reasons. The first was that there was nothing anyone else could do. She found it a waste of time to confide in someone who in no way could improve the conditions of her tragedies. They walk away knowing and she boards the same train back. Second, she hated the ten seconds of awkwardness that followed when she said what hurt her enough to end her life, which involved someone nodding, a fake sentiment or two, the beeping of a distant garbage truck, and the scrambling, impossible transition to something else. Lastly, it was her disdain for feeling stolen—that revealing her sensitivity was an opportunity for someone else to profit. To take *all that was her* and use her life as a thought experiment. *Oh god, oh no. I am possessive of my own pain,* the waitress thought. Her hands covered her face. *Isn't that fucked up? Aren't we supposed to learn from each other? Why am I like this? But truly, please, answer me God, am I wrong? I don't want people. They use you to better themselves. Of course, I want people to live happy lives, but don't… take… me! I am all I have. I don't want people, God. And they stay for too long. Is there not something mistrustful in connection—that by keeping people in our life, we're mistakenly trying to create an equation that does not prove? But no,* she remembered. *I miss Craig.* And with the memory of Craig, she held onto him gently, as though for dear life, as she did time and time again. She knew that at least once in her life, her expressions proved equal.

And last, there stood an empty chair. And the vacant table, too, in front of it. It would have belonged to a particular someone, but they were too afraid to come. The air conditioning cooled the wood. The stranger not there found social goings disappointing and lived in fear at home.

People avoided that chair.

No one wanted to sit there. Then it was where Andrei sat.

7
THE AGENCY

Before the shop served coffee and pastries, it was an office space belonging to a group of hard-working talent agents.

This was a few decades ago, and the agency repped a few recognizable names in television, but mostly focused on a roster of developmental clients. They would scout drama schools in Los Angeles and New York and once signing them, would send their actors out to audition. The agency launched careers for some of the most talented young actors coming out of conservatories. So little of the café resembled the agency, except for the curtains.

For the sake of tradition, or laziness on behalf of the management, the coffee shop had kept the green curtains that were stitched to the ceiling when sold. They were first hung up by Bradford Keller, head agent. He was a kind, handsome man of medium height with gray-blue eyes. He gelled his blond hair every morning, upwards and to the right, and sprayed it twice for extra hold. Bradford did not exercise or lift weights, but his shoulders were broad and he kept his neck erect and so with the right shirt, he normally passed for fit. Bradford had enthusiastically started the company with two colleagues and while he had the skills of a great agent, he was most known for presentation.

Bradford dressed the company's office in the reputation he wanted associated with the agency: organized, regal, and proper. He had an intuition for creating impressions. It was a remarkable, crafty talent: an amalgamation of senses for timing, design, drama, and people. In some of his larger negotiations with producers, he would have his colleagues say scripted lines in the background such as, "Third call today! Kathy booked another pilot, clear to close?" and succeed in making his clients look more desirable. Bradford was filled with bold plays and cunning strategies that inspired everyone around him. He understood the power of appearance. And this meant everything from the weight of the front door pushed to enter to the color of ink agents signed contracts with. The space was small and all that the ambitious three colleagues could afford, but Keller's eye for décor was nonetheless exquisite. The first thing he needed, however, was a green curtain. This was not any ordinary green curtain.

"They must be in velvet," he repeated over the telephone. "And I'd like two sets, fifty-two by ninety-six inches. Dark green." And he closed his eyes and remembered the green he needed:

Bradford started his twenties taking trains up and down France. He gripped the metal handling above his head and was filled all over with the prickling sensation of awareness and energy one feels abroad. He was headed to Lyon and observed how men stood up and gave their seats to women. He looked around and to his side felt a thoughtful glance from a woman his age. The twenty-year-old French woman had astonishingly long, brown hair and powerful legs. She wore a two-piece suit of striking green. The green conjured a rich hue that sucked in light as if it were a cave, but in seconds, as light moved, dazzled his eyes with emerald.

Keller and the woman exchanged a polite smile and proceeded to look in different directions. The whole ride, they danced with gestures. Bradford would study the reflection of her face from the window in front of her and once pleased, he would look away as if to pass the baton and say, *your turn.* And she took it. The woman enjoyed his build and arms and eyelashes. She would turn to break her glance casually away and run her fingers through her hair, remembering the American man as if he were already a memory. Bradford's cues were endless. He rolled up his sleeves. He let out a cough to share another peek. If there was the slightest noise in her direction, he would make an excuse to face curiously there. She was slightly limited by her seated position, but managed to follow after him, with her body attuned to her thoughts. She crossed her legs to prompt his curiosity of sudden movement. She spoke politely to an old lady for him to see. She saw how he wore green, too—a different pale, forest green sweater—but nonetheless green like hers!—and she loaded that stupid comment of matching clothes in her throat, should there ever be a window to fire. The climax was when the two seemingly searching, thinking, would look *just* around the other person, daring as close as an inch, but never directly. They soaked each other up in their peripheral views.

He knew these things and felt them, but one could never be so sure. He could have been overly imaginative. Too attentive. Despite the subtle language they shared, nothing was indeed admitted with words. Yet an extraordinary moment of profound hope happened that Bradford Keller would remember in sadness for the rest of his life. When a Frenchman rushed passionately past with his suitcase toward the door, he knocked Bradford's sunglasses to the ground. It was with a dull thud nobody heard, against a slowing train preparing for its stop. And as soon as his frames hit the floor, the woman in green's hand shot out so quickly that she blew her cover. Her beautiful, healthy arm reached far forward, an uncomfortable distance made to look effortless. Even the man reading next to the lady was startled by her sudden maneuver. She was patient, but brisk, as if waiting all along for a reason to make contact. It was not a reach of politeness. It was a reach that held the hour. That was why her arm communicated what it did; the French girl in green had not been minding her own business and suddenly interrupted by a noise. She had been thinking about him. And praying for a bridge. And when she crossed it, it happened as such:

"Ah, *monsieur*," said the lady in green. She offered her hand to him, holding his leopard print shades.

Bradford, being too shy in a foreign country, barely looked at her.

"*Merci!*" he thanked, telling everyone around them, but not her.

She reached for his blue eyes, but only found his averting white. Bradford's hand squeezed the rail above his head.

The woman in green noticed the next stop was hers. She contemplated staying and skipping her *stage,* but whether she got up to leave would not matter should the American man have the courage to stop her. The train came to a halt, and she walked ever so slowly toward the door, waiting for a *pardon.*

She could barely breathe after such an intense ride. They were both so concentrative in their individual composure it was almost lunacy.

"*Excusez-moi, mademoiselle! Pardon*—" imagined the girl.

But instead she heard his regret, and the doors that closed behind her. The whistles of a machine moving further and further took Bradford Keller away and that away was forever.

Bradford's hand kept slipping from the rail. His sweat loosened his grip. He had wanted to say something to her but felt he was so out of place. *I'm pathetic and stupid. She must ride the train every day,* he said to himself. *I'd disturb her! Why am I anything special? People feel romantic on trains and buses all the time… I was just imagining things.* Bradford accepted his incredulity. But one image banged on the doors of his mind like a crazy villager who knows the truth and cannot be suppressed. One, single memory kept flashing back: her nimble hand. It had stretched out like lightning.

Her arm. And that hand! Oh, that hand. What could life have been had I followed that hand? he would cry. Why did Keller not trust her hand? *The timing of her reach was crystal clear! There could be no surer giveaway!* These thoughts tortured him and he was filled to the brim with remorse. Bradford had all of France before him begging to be explored. Though the young agent mapped out a long list of chapels to visit and prayed on his knees for the same thing: that the woman in green had an amazing life with a man who had the courage to stop her from leaving. *We will never have each other. No wedding. No future. No kids. But that day,* he said to himself, *that delicate hand went up for me. Me.* And he thanked the saints for giving him that. *An average life span of a short eighty years—and to at least be the reason she once moved? Thank you.*

And he could keep the color forever. Colors, songs, clothes, and receipts—objects of the earth were kept when they could not keep people.

Bradford would love that rich shade of green as if it were her. And when the curtain order came to the agency, he sent it back. It was not dark enough. And when it was dark enough, it was not green enough. And if it were everything, something would be missing. So he opened back the phone book to call the company.

"I want the direct line to your manufacturer, whatever the cost," he said.

And with his charisma and persuasiveness, he locked in a deal with the factory to test ship various prints. Over the span of eighteen months, Keller would pay $49.95 per shipment containing a custom sample fabric until eventually one morning he stood on a ladder and installed the woman in green's green.

Some nights, Bradford would lean back on his swivel chair and hold the emerald velvet close to his cheeks. That explained the wear and tear near the bottom.

And this was why the curtains were green.

For the most part, the café had been considerably remodeled. But like with all rooms, human history hid, lingering in the air like cigarette smoke rebellious children try to quickly fan, but touches every wall and object inside.

Remnants of the old agency lived everywhere in the café. A spitball had dried in one corner of the room from one of Bradford's playful colleagues. Champagne had stained two whole tiles of the ceiling when the company celebrated its first major motion picture booking. Most special of all was a subtle dent in the wall—the history being a frustrated, young intern who had thrown her small fist with as much force as privacy could afford. That intern was Chelsea.

One day Chelsea was especially anxious because the agency was in mayhem from all the college showcases. Numerous meetings with new talent blocked the week and of course, they gave all the work to the intern. She looked for new showcases, attended them, and scheduled the meetings. That day, Chelsea would coordinate the sign-in for actors arriving to meet with the agents. She was excellent at her job and hired especially for her great people skills, but once in a while, certain young men would come in and Chelsea would behave so strangely around them. If a pretty boy entered the office, her eyes froze to ice and her voice invented a stoic nature. It was unrecognizable.

She hated this characteristic of hers. It was simply so weird to her. Chelsea was raised by her parents to be respectful. She had handled countless high-pressure situations at the agency and in school. The girl loved her internship, and her dream was to be a producer, so she felt that working with talent agents would give her a solid introduction to show business. But certain men who looked gentle, she hated. Every time they came near to make light conversation, she would make it a point to show them her back. Chelsea wanted to sting them. She would turn her body in a mean, exerting force that said: *Look at me, I am facing the other way! Feel it! Be hurt!*

There lived in Chelsea a complicated knot of feelings toward the opposite gender. She had pleasant features, ambition, and wonderful athleticism. Throughout her education, she drew in many immature boys. They were cruel and self-obsessed, which was common at that age, and never satisfied her wants. She focused on her studies and would become exceptionally smart. However, the young girl held off a little too long. By the time she finished high school, she had not had her first kiss. And by the time she finished graduating college, she had never had a boyfriend. Chelsea grew worried of her inexperience. Consequently, her need for a boy who could treat her well, understand her, and hold her true, was exceedingly high. This need became so important to her and because of this citadel, she grew fearful whenever someone came close. If she let the wrong prince into her castle, Chelsea would be destroyed from within and have to reconstruct her kingdom all over again. If any gentleman was near enough to make Chelsea nervous, she would cast them out—in disbelief of their potential goodness and insecurity of her lack of experience. Her coldness and gestures of indifference were her way of saying, *You're not real. But if you are, you'll disappoint me. Or you will reject me. So I will give you my back and hurt you before you hurt me, perfect man.* The longer Chelsea was alone, the higher her standards grew. And the more she wanted love, the less prepared she was to have it.

Before the agency closed for the day, one final actor waited patiently for his meeting. His dark skin glistened from the California sunset peering through the glass block windows. He wore a fitted suit. His legs were folded, revealing salmon argyle socks, and he struck up a lovely conversation with Chelsea. The actor came off so calm that her customary guards were not let up. His innocent demeanor was nothing but friendly and he managed to sneak up on her in the most charming way. They laughed in pink jazz and talked like champagne without ever drinking it. The agents called him in and he excused himself. Chelsea, alone, found herself blushing at the memory of him. She looked at his chair and wanted to slide her hands over the seat. She traced his signature on her sign-in clipboard with her own pen. The first thing they would do, she imagined, would be a date at Griffith.

But then wicked time set in and darkened her merry heart to a doubtful plum. Chelsea remembered her indestructible alcazar and took a deep breath.

Once his meeting was over, the actor returned to her little desk to pick up where they left off. And like an alarm setting off inside her, Chelsea abruptly picked up her ballpoint pen, scribbled some meaningless note in a book, and flatly told the page, "Thank you for coming in. Best of luck to you."

The actor blinked, hurt. He felt that chilly world of duplicity—having been given her benevolence and now her indifference. Few things burned men as much as the cold side of a woman that was once warm. They'd had her once, right in their hands, but now that woman had insensibly disappeared. *Will I ever know her again? What have I done? God, how she flipped her warmth altogether like a switch! I hate not knowing her anymore,* he thought. The actor tried to meet her eyes, but accepted from her composure she would not be kindled. He lifted his hand and rested his grateful, sad fingers on the edge of the table as if her hand were there. They both watched him squeeze her tabletop gently, how he brushed his thumb side to side, and then released. The proper boy smiled, stood firmly, and exited slowly out the door.

He wasn't interested in me. He only talked to me to be polite. Or for me to put in a good word. In fact, he was probably nervous and just using our conversation as a way to release his nerves. That's all, she told herself. But when his meeting was over, Chelsea remembered that hand and what it had done. How it had traveled to his end of the table. The way his wrist had rested. How his fingers had lingered on the wood as he left. Chelsea failed herself once more and felt as if her towers were so high in the air, she could never jump down. And it was growing taller and taller—and her life was getting shorter and shorter—and she still had no one and no one.

She rushed to the back of the agency, unsure of why she loved to kill love, and crying, punched the wall.

"Hey! Everything okay?" said Bradford Keller, hearing a thud from his desk.

"Yes. Just knocked into something."

"Okay. Don't hurt yourself."

Chelsea's dent hid behind an espresso machine, which was beside a row of fresh coffee beans in glass jars. A stack of paper cups and lids towered tall next to it.

The café was open Monday through Friday from 7 a.m. to 9 p.m. and Saturday and Sunday from 8 a.m. to 5 p.m. Pets welcome. Premium public Wi-Fi available. And the key to the restroom was a code that could be found at the right of the register.

8

THE HOTEL

Andrei paced in front of the hotel, his heart pounding.
"Okay," he said. "Let's do this."

His eyes darted to the grand staircase that shined at the entrance. Silver bell carts were lined up beside the valet booth. Lengthy, green vines hugged the entrance's walls and suddenly, a chrome sports car had pulled up. Andrei watched the passengers crawl out of a single vehicle.

How the hell did that many women fit inside a car like that? he thought.

One assumed working at a hotel desk was nice. The uniform. The air conditioning. The cleanliness. The gold. And most of all, the hundreds of beautiful people who walked past every day. And they would be right. The atmosphere was splendid. And it was captivating to compare the differences and subtleties of people and all that could happen in a standard check-in. One man who was asked to sign a receipt might have snatched the pen out of Andrei's pocket and given his rough signature in such a confident way it somehow inspired admiration. A woman entering might have worn a less promiscuous dress than her showy girlfriends but was far more intriguing and left Andrei wondering why. Tension within a marriage might have erupted in a heated argument at Andrei's check-in desk where he could do nothing but stand there awkwardly. In other couples, he grew attuned to the slightest, charged comments, perhaps of bringing too much luggage, that indicated an imminent separation. Scents, shapes, accents, personalities, and the sheer numbers of all of the above passed him like a bullet train, and he, the civilian, whose duty it was to stand still.

And after some months, the exposure to beauty and wealth took a toll on his mind. He could not pinpoint it at first. Andrei thought human change came from decisions, but actually it came from observation. For example, in one war-torn part of the world, there was a child who watched a building collapse on his brother, so he fell unconscious to the ground. When he woke up, he could no longer talk. The boy lost his voice. Certainly, yes, people changed, but mostly, people *were changed*. In other cases, some healthcare workers never slept the same. After treating mangled human bodies, witnessing infants abducted, and spending sleep hours to calm violent patients, something broke in a nurse that no pillow could fix. Working at the hotel caused no mere day-job fatigue, but with careful regard was as dramatic as shell shock. The brain was a special piano whose song history was never forgotten; one wrong key could destroy the instrument and necessitate years of healing. For Andrei, the multitude of wealthy guests, their walks, accommodation requests, secrets, women, and jewels had achieved his natural lust for luxury ten times over and turned him into a complete ghost.

And this ghost believed he was in the last phase of life. He considered his anesthesia an inevitable chapter of a human being. After a certain amount of naked bodies, blood on the walls, and vomit on the floor, the color white will look gray. Once he surrendered to gray, the uncaring world proved his worldview. He walked the sunny streets and knew no passerby would ever save him from his rainstorm. He could cry all the way to work and back unstopped. The unconcern of the world confirmed to him that he was a ghost, not only because he was deadened from the hotel, but because when he left and stepped outside it, he knew, indisputably, everyone else was dead to everyone else. To be alive is to play the role of ghost.

The job position the boy held made him doubt that there was any kind of goodness left in men and women. Even the women he met whose character seemed so fortified had turned out to break vows while their partners drank at the bar. Additionally, how many angels could a man let walk past him without wanting to jump up, save one, and fly away with them? *But save them for what?* he asks. *For another hotel room and perform the same evil? I'm a phony.* He tended to close his eyes around good-looking women out of respect. But the urge to wrap his arms around them was still there. Anytime Andrei saw an attractive girl, he felt puny. *I'm so far from her,* he thinks, *we are impossible. Just look at the legs and you know.*

When women showed him a sign, he crushed it— viewing their offer as a villainous trap. He had killed many futures at his desk and did not understand it himself. In him was an impulsive, reckless lever he pulled to crush innocence he did not want to ruin by finding out was illusion. It was only natural. At one point, a young woman even asked Andrei on a date directly and he was moved by her sweetness. Then remembering himself, and the women who escaped to strangers' rooms, the agent looked her straight in the eye with genius violence and told her he had a girlfriend. *Kill the heart,* he repeated to himself. He was vengeful. He was really saying, *"I hate you so much that I'll destroy myself and all that I love! Which is you!"*

A resistant heart wanted and expected to be stopped. But few were curious enough to understand the blizzard behind a "no." He stared unaffectedly at the women who walked past, adoring them from inside. And before dawn, when the city was quiet and mournful, and a window in Andrei might have opened to let love inside, he heard giggles from a distance and a large arm would wrap itself around the stumbling angels who wore heels, pulling them harshly toward the glossy elevator, grunting "My room, now!" and Andrei would wince at the sound of their feet clicking toward the room of monsters.

Plenty of evil happened inside that building. One may encourage Andrei to cheer up, that it was only the building:

"Don't sweat it, man. It isn't real. That's only one part of the world," assured Andrei's co-workers on his first week.

But it was real. I mean, it was upstairs for Christ's sake. "And one part of the world," Andrei said to himself, "is still *of* the world."

It was too easy to try and remedy depression by widening one's perspective and proclaiming there were a million other avenues in which to see life. It did not change the fact that such hotels existed. Hotels with affairs. Abuse. Drugs that scared. All of this told him that people did not sit on grass fields, melting under the sun, sacrificing their afternoons with friends to love. Instead, they purchased king suites with escorts and ordered wagyu rare.

Andrei had had his fair share of wagyu. The employee discount served him well at the bar and restaurant. When he outgrew the selection, he ventured out. It took more and more for new restaurants to impress him. The choice of lighting. The weight of the utensils. The quality of the tablecloth. The truffle. He looked at upscale menus and searched miserably for some hidden dish. *What more can you do to chicken?* He flipped menus to see the alcohol list. *This wine and that go down the same hole and wait, how different can pan-seared truly be?* He, born poor, had quickly exhausted his gluttonous curiosities after spending time in splendor. Everything had been exhausted.

This was why he returned to the hotel to ask the old actress some more questions.

When off the clock, the front desk agent was not allowed back inside the hotel. The union protected him in such a way that once his shift was over, he was not permitted on property under any circumstance, even if it was to pick up a jacket he'd forgotten. Andrei had to craft a way to sneak up to the Mars' floor without getting caught.

A disguise was out of the question. Andrei knew it could not be pulled off. The two bellmen in the front were trained thoroughly to greet and make eye contact with every guest who entered. And there was no way of climbing the back gate because of the cameras. And he could not use the employee entrance on the side because the punch-in code used to unlock the door would procedurally alert security, who approved every staff entry. There was only one option.

"Overtime!" he yelled, waving to the valet.

Andrei jogged urgently toward the parking garage, where the attendants nodded to him.

"Get that money, brotha!" said one of them, as Andrei entered the shadowed lot. He passed a row of electric cars at their respective charging stations, a string of black SUVs designated for private security details, and an assortment of rented supercars and convertibles.

Once inside, the intruder regained his breath. Andrei had never broken in anywhere. He felt an adrenaline new to him, like his pulse was actually doing its job for once. He pulled open a metal door and walked up the fire escape.

The garage led to a stairwell entrance to the lobby, where he faced the only elevator with access to guests' rooms. But in the elevator, dual surveillance cameras were mounted to the ceiling. There was also the chance that once in the lift, he would run into one of his managers, a bellman, or a guest like Mr. Cohen, who would probably announce somehow to a receptionist that he'd just seen his greatest companion.

Wait no, he thought. *That's not the only one. In-room dining has their own service elevator. I can take it straight up. But that's in the kitchen, where I'd have to cross straight through the lobby. And that's too high of a risk.*

Andrei was stumped. But he could not contemplate for too long. Anyone could spot him. Andrei walked discreetly to the restroom and hid inside a stall. There was an Impressionist painting above the toilet. *For a shit machine, these things smell so good.*

He paced up and down the small.

How could he meet Mars? He could wait for the woman to go outside, but she may never do that. He needed to speak with her *now*.

He listened to the gas and groans of bloated men for ten minutes. By nature, there were more toilet flushes in the men's restroom than sink usage. Suddenly a wave of chatter flooded the washroom. Kids, dressed for a swim at the pool, barged noisily into the stalls. He felt a spark of chance. He did not know how the group could help him, but knew standing there was fruitless and was determined to cast his fishing rod in random waters. Andrei acted quickly.

Exiting his stall, he calmly went over to the sink. The kids were in their early teens, mostly the scrawny kind nearly his height.

"Where you guys headed?" asked Andrei.

"Don't you see my swim trunks?" said a tall, blond boy.

"Yes," said Andrei.

"So where do you think?"

"The pool?"

"This guy's a genius!" The kids laughed.

Rich kids were the worst, thought Andrei. But they were so bad that Andrei's plan might work.

"What's your name?" asked Andrei.

"My name?"

"Isn't that what I asked?" The group snickered.

"Yeah."

"Did you forget?"

"It's Brett."

Andrei smiled. Of course it was. Andrei always thought there was a fundamental eeriness to names. If a name had an adorable ring to it, like Bonnie or Milo, it was cute to say and hard to be angry at a Bonnie for long. People treated others the way their names sounded. If someone's name was common, people would mostly see neutral characters—shy, kind, or good-natured. If one's name was unusual, people had lazier associations and treated them as either a spectacle or an artist. If their name was a title commanding presence, the world's reaction to them, however subtle, would naturally endow them with a confidence as easily handed to them as their name.

He saw it in other ways, like beauty. People *acted* how they looked like. The reactions of the world to one's appearance were an invisible estimation of one's perception of themselves. The beautiful and the hideous each got treated a certain way—experiencing wildly different kinds of years. The beautiful were told phrases the hideous never heard. The beautiful struggled more with envy, while the hideous spent more time practicing courage, for things never easily bent their way. Every person accepted how they were treated and sank into that role. It showed in the way they sat. How their heads turn. When they spoke. If they spoke. Mannerisms were then not a matter of individual personality, but collective decree. Andrei would notice in a stranger all the things their body did, memorize them, and project them imaginarily on a different person. The imagined transference would never work! It seemed odd, like a miscalculation, to visualize a gorgeous Adonis walk with his head down and fidgety fingers the way a shy man did. There was undeniably a pattern of traits between strangers, courtesy of the strangers *they* meet.

The actress upstairs, however, was the only person Andrei had ever met who seemed to defy her shell. The old woman never acted as if she was pigeonholed into an identity or appearance. Of course she was beautiful, but she was attached to nothing and her body followed *her*. With this thought, another round of feelings in Andrei burned to see her again. He continued with his plan.

Andrei stared at the pawn to his scheme. Brett.

This blond Brett boy was very tall. And in his disposition seemed an incompleteness. People who talked to Brett usually first referenced his height. Thus, a compliment or statement regarding his figure was the first thing he heard. Andrei could imagine that the first fraction of every conversation in his life had to do with how tall he was. And since conversations did not last that long, Brett had mastered the form of receiving the compliment, but compared to folks with a shorter body, had a considerably lower percentage of conversations in his life about other things. It was merely the way it had turned out. The world acknowledged Brett's height and Brett monopolized this attention and innocently adjusted by mentioning his height for all sorts of topics—for being the butt of jokes, for flirtation, to compete in the quiet dance of masculine dominance in rooms that men knew so well. Andrei located the offness to him—a certain naïve, boyish way Brett spoke and moved. If Andrei and Brett had been the same age, not in a hotel restroom, and most importantly, friends, Andrei would have offered him some advice: "Accept comments on your height quickly, my friend, and then never address it again. Change the topic fast and carry on. You don't want to lose out on the higher picture." And the same words would apply to every living thing: "Rather than be swayed, strike through everything you do. Your mighty sword is your identity, not mirrors, reflections, or other eyeballs."

"Okay, Brett. I bet you I can swim faster than you."

"You wanna bet?"

"I just said that I bet."

His friends howled and he was at a loss for words. Brett blushed. They egged him on.

"Dude, I'm six three," said Brett.

"And that's just about all you are, huh?" *It felt good to talk to a guest like that.*

"How much?"

"Let's just shake on it. We bet on pride."

"Fine with me."

Andrei's plans were in motion. Now all he had to do was cross straight through the lobby.

"We need a referee," commanded Andrei.

Then, all the boys chimed in roughly, raising their hands. They shoved each other toward the center until Andrei announced the conditions to the shirtless pack.

"We all race to the pool. First one there gets to call it—count off me and Brett." The teens lit up. "We cut through the lobby, past the spa…" *where right down the hall will be the kitchen entrance,* he said to himself, "…then past the fitness deck and we'll cannonball straight into the pool. Brett, first one to touch the water wins."

The boys cheered upon his instructions, pumping their chests, and began to stretch.

"We start on the wall. Everyone—HEY! On the wall! At least one hand on it."

The kids extended their arms to the black tiled ceramic, with excited looks. A few boys on the side giggled. Andrei removed his work uniform until he was shirtless and held it in his arm.

"Why don't you lead the countdown, Brett?"

"Three."

They breathed.

"Two."

Andrei smiled.

"One… GO!"

Laughter burst out of the bathroom. The boys sprinted on the glossy, onyx floor, tackling the door open. They were beginning to cross through the lobby when Andrei shifted his position to the center.

"Please, no running. HEY, NO RUNNING!" yelled an employee. Andrei recognized his manager's voice and continued on, hidden in the shuffle of his innocent conspirators.

The shirtless pack responded with screeches, skids, and squeaks, battling for triumph under a shaking chandelier. A surge of wind blew past the lobby. Once they made it through, Andrei slackened his speed and jogged behind one of the boys on the side. The giggling group shoved each other as they ran, squeezing amongst themselves in the tight hallway toward the sauna. Brett accelerated to the front, en route to superiority. Unnoticed, Andrei slipped away from the others and launched himself into the kitchen.

The large, smoky room carried hoarse shouting. It buzzed with sizzles, chopping, timers, and frying. No one seemed to notice the intruder, but for safety, he hugged the side and made his way carefully to the private service elevator.

Once it dinged, he entered inside. *Finally.*

"Corner!" said one of the servers.

The worker held a busy plate of alcohol, lobster mac and cheese, and miso cod. The foodrunner jumped into the elevator and saw a shirtless trespasser standing awkwardly.

The server pressed the button hesitantly up to the seventh floor and looked at Andrei.

"I… uh…. I'm here for an interview," Andrei said.

"I've seen you like six times, brah."

"Oh."

"Ha, yeah."

Andrei gulped. He eyed the food tray and was impressed at its array.

"Do you ever drop food?" he asked the server.

"Yo, it's crazy you ask that 'cause I've been here two years and all the guys do, even today man you should've seen it, but me, I've never—oh wait actually there was this one time at another job—"

And suddenly, the lift shook to a stop.

"Oh shit I gotta go, I'll tell you later—peace, papi!"

Andrei saluted goodbye and went up to Mars' floor in good spirits. Four-two-five. He knocked on her door. While waiting, he remembered his nipples were out and buttoned his shirt back on. He slid his arms through his blazer and knocked a second time.

Nothing.

C'mon, where is she?

After a moment, the old actress swung the door open and, without ever glancing at the boy, gestured him inside and walked back into the room. Then, as if there had been no time in between, no questions on her part, she continued their conversation casually, navigating through the suite she'd now made her own.

"You asked me about Hollywood and I thought about it—"

"What did you mean by 'like a comet'?"

"Come again?"

"What did you mean when you said it? Earlier, you said 'like a comet.' What's that mean?"

It was here that she would give Andrei his mission. Mars believed the one thing worth chasing after was to be outside one's own humanity, which was in this case to be more than human and as a result, be rid of any imposed fear. There was one type of lifestyle, however, that naturally encompassed this way of living, she explained.

"Celebrity," said Mars.

She explained how the famous had enough wealth to cheat courage. They could see all the corners of the earth. They indulged in lavish tastes and were surrounded by enough praising crowds to convince them of deserving an attitude of greatness they did not actually build on their own. The famous could say what they wanted and had the valor to speak to any stranger on the street because they themselves were not strangers on the street. The sidewalks bowed to them. These types of humans were not better than others, but would unmistakably live and have more than the average person. Celebrity was a cunning occupation and a sneaky style of living that unlocked an extraordinary life.

She sat crisscrossed on her bed and capped her colored highlighters that spread over her script.

"But not all people can be rich and famous," she insisted. Mars stressed her enunciation, and spoke emphatically, as if giving vital orders to military personnel and continued: "And that goes away once people stop giving you attention. So the only other option for us would be to make the terrifying, but sensible choice of living like a comet. An unstoppable rock through space. Traveling with so great a speed that there is no time or desire for explanation. You live. You live without brakes."

His heart raced. Andrei shifted his gear to second. This was his key.

The spine of an upstanding life was character. If all else was rid of, that was all a human had. The decisions in one's own identity was like the wardrobe of the spirit, as discussed by Mars and Andrei. If a human being was fearless, she told him, they would act on all the things they desired. They would speak all the thoughts they were afraid to say. This pulled them closer to the sublime and away from obvious lands. Their life would gain access to moments of intimacy that were never far—only camouflaged. There was no one Andrei knew who lived like that. Not one. The comet was the most optimal way of life. Nothing could stop the person who decided to nail their foot on the gas. No interaction, rejection, weather, or obstacle of any kind would arrest them for too long. Everyone else had delays and was set back by their excuses.

"Tea?" she asked.

"Please."

Mars filled the kettle with sink water and boiled two cups of green tea. She tapped a nice amount of sugar into the steam and walked over with two mugs to Andrei who was seated on her couch. They sipped in tandem.

"But *imagine,*" said Mars, "being a comet. I want you to imagine a divine force in someone that pushes them through the world, infinitely, in each choice, melting barriers in its own perfect path, out your mouth, out from your hands, across countries, through rooms—"

"—through terror—"

"—past regulations—"

"—past people—"

"—every time—"

"—every day…"

"Their life would go so much further," continued Mars, "so much—as if absorbing hundreds and hundreds of years of ordinary life experience while still their real age. If death is no secret, why do we hunch? That doesn't make sense to me. I don't get the hunching! We retreat even when we always know the most favorable thing to do. If you took every risk, you'd have everything. You'd have all that was all."

"I understand. Though I'm afraid that kind of perspective requires bravery. And I'm not brave. I'm alone."

Mars paused. She looked at the boy in her room and said:

"Once you go, you're off. The rest is momentum. You don't feel the shakes at that speed."

"What's your name, again?" he asked.

"Mars. A pleasure to meet you…"

"Andrei. But, Mars…" he said. He put down his cup and scooted close to her. He got under her eyes and splurted: "I can thank you, but you wouldn't understand how hard I've been searching. I don't want to pity myself, but the past few years, I felt I was living in the arctic and there's nothing more to me than this. In other words. I'd take off a fingernail for it."

"I understand," said Mars. Watching his outpour was like watching a clown—not in a goofy way, but in an honest illustration of transparency that Mars valued.

"But I must ask—how do you know you're ready?" he said.

"You are ready because you're here," she said.

Andrei listened so closely he nearly got dizzy.

"You're here. And you've been looking for something. I saw it as soon as I caught you masturbating in front of that wall."

"Well, you didn't catch me masturbating—"

"No, I did. I was standing right there."

"But I heard the door open."

"I re-opened and closed it for you to hide. It was so exciting. You were so in it. You didn't even hear me come in the first time!" Mars laughed, clasping her hands, wiggling to the side. She got such pleasure from happenings, especially in the ones she stirred herself for amusement.

"But listen, Andrei. You found me. That's why you're ready. If you weren't, we would not have met. This is how missions start and end: the second its hero already has it within him. We know that from the five-act structure, from plays, from movies—it's in the script. We earn our encounters. That's why you are ready."

They made another cup of tea and delighted in the conversation of the comet for a while.

This is what Andrei wanted. He saw his own comet so clearly. If he chose to, the boy could strike through all his terrors, any small trivial conflicts, blazing on his own accord. Unyielding. Ever flowing. Unfaltering.

Warriors did not slay dragons with their hands in their pockets—a swing must be made. As such, the only way to live with a sense of victory was to make an attempt every time it was asked for. One could climb the ranks of life swiftly through every choice, through every conversation, by never hesitating. *Oh, where that streak could take you!* And if mistakes were made, moping was no option. There was only ever forward for comets. Andrei believed that only good things could come of this navigation and desired to start.

Mars saw that.

"And so now. Listen to yourself. Tune in. What do you want?'

"What do I want?" he repeated.

He thought. And instantly, he knew. Andrei's heart pounded while the suite was still. In fact, it was the type of stillness that men and women knew all too well. That familiar, embarrassing calm, which in seconds usually soared an unquestionable fact. Minds in that room could only come to the single conclusion Andrei feared to admit.

"I want to…" And Andrei, taking Mars' hands in his, bent over and kissed her with an angle of awe and the timing of gratitude.

"Right," she said, knowingly.

"Did you know I was going to do that? Was that weird?"

"Why explain feelings, Andrei?" she professed sincerely. "We'll end up dissatisfied. If you feel the truth, so do I. That's how rooms work. You have to keep doing that. Listening carefully, then acting fiercely. It's a contrasting relationship."

Her phone rang.

"I am so sorry, Andrei." Mars walked toward her phone. He read her look and knew she needed to take it. But that was her comet. And she was slipping rightly through the earth in her own unpredictable, heroic fashion. She could be anything anywhere. And today, she taught Andrei he could too. He watched her worked-up hands hold the phone.

"Thank you," he said.

Mars' hands gestured over her heart, then erratically motioning, clenched, and moved out excitedly toward Andrei, as if capturing some unspoken feeling in her and pouring it in his direction.

"BAH!"

Andrei laughed and approached the door. He closed it shut, not understanding what she did, but feeling exactly what she meant.

Holding onto feelings was far more delicate than holding onto words. Feelings were carried, like invisible fairies caught by chance in the woodlands that one holds in their hand, and feels its weight, but cannot see. They were ethereal, exclusively and tenderly known to the people involved, and usually deeper and more colorful than speech, but more prone to extinction from doubt. Words, alternatively, could be written down, were easy to remember, and worked well for stories—but they limited feelings by nature and could be exaggerated or confused by newer words. Andrei held the memory of Mars and saved the feelings they exchanged over their words. This was no simple conversation. It was a break-and-entry. A kiss of need. A rope to safety. An exposure to greatness. A flare in the dark.

He left the hotel through the front door.

9
THE GARDEN

A ndrei climbed down the front staircase and eager to reach the bottom, jumped down to the ground. He looked up and felt his brain throw itself a yard ahead and propel time. He stumbled against the railing, his vision blurring and head thumping.

"Ah," he moaned. Andrei raised his hands to his faint temples and frowned.

Andrei's feet did not normally jump down the stairs when he left work. They walked through the employee gate, carefully down a ramp in a walkway—avoiding any spillage from the restaurant—and paced leisurely to fulfill a routine his body had memorized down to the very sequence of steps. Whenever he went outside, his brain auto-piloted his regimen—imagining the drilled path he always took: a left on Hilgard, straight down Le Conte, then a right at Gayley Avenue. But some new formation inside Andrei had broken his traditional trace. At that moment, his mind panged and he forgot how to go home.

He took a few seconds to breathe and regained himself.

Andrei could walk the path that led from his workplace to his apartment. But tuning in to his comet, and his zeal to stretch life, the memory of Mars inspired him to forge a new path. Andrei would go directly home. And to him, *directly* meant *straight*. A complete, direct, linear course forward. He would dispatch from this street and not take any turns, never bending, never leaning, and would march as straight as an arrow.

Setting his eyes ahead, he cut through the road before a passing car and sprinted toward his first obstacle. He faced a lofty fence, which guarded a botanical garden. Chains wrapped around the entrance gate like tough snakes who'd lost to Medusa. So Andrei put his foot on those snakes first and pulled himself up to the very top, where protruding metals poked his palms painfully. It was not an option for him to turn his body and procedurally climb down. His hands could bleed at any time now. The trespasser had to jump.

Seize the future as soon as it flashes, he said to himself.

And without a moment's hesitation, Andrei launched himself up and fell to the ground, crashing right on a family of little stones. But he was okay. His body was stronger than he thought.

Onwards.

He saw the garden's curved path and was tempted to enjoy the scenery. But his biker instincts helped reinforce his comet. Andrei neglected the visitor's trail and trekked straight ahead.

Andrei hiked through tall grasses, squeezed in between bamboo trees, and bouldered his way up rocky hills. His forehead began to moisten and his chest rose higher and higher. He stopped when faced with a stream of water dividing the garden. *How far am I willing to go?* he thought. He dipped his Oxfords in the mossy blue and sent himself straight through the river, where turtles spectated his strangeness. Andrei laughed loudly as he crossed the cold, knee-deep, giggling not only out of humor but as a natural mechanism to withstand the chill.

One little baby turtle swam gracefully toward him.

Andrei reached out and picked it up with his hands and grazed its shell. It was the first time he'd noticed such mesmerizing sea patterns. He focused on all the varying shades of green that blended into its skin. Soon, no less than a dozen turtles started to make their way toward him, so he rushed out of the water and continued through the leaves that vibrated ahead.

The set path taken by most garden visitors would have ensured incredible sights. One would be able to read the titles and descriptions of plants, never miss a single species of tree, and would never have to worry about soaked shoes.

But on his trail, the soaked-shoed boy saw a side to the garden hidden from its guests.

When passing directly under the lilac trees, a gust of wind pushed forth a scent of fresh sweetness that could only have been known to the seduced animals directly under. And when Andrei had to push through tall stalks of plants, unable to see ahead of himself, he interrupted the sleep of a colony of bugs laying so colorfully on a leaf one would confuse them for berries! And when laboriously cutting through seemingly dull rocks the size of tires, Andrei peeked inside the dark crevices to find hatchlings flapping their excited wings as they bathed from a spring. His diagonal odyssey tingled his feet and gifted him an extraordinary excursion.

Andrei reached the perimeter of the garden. Once he climbed over the fence, the drop being easier that time around, he landed at a corner of the university.

To his left, he could take the next blue bus that would take students through campus and stop across the street from his home. To his right, Andrei saw a construction ramp leading to the center of the university and eventually his apartment—but these were left and right. Andrei had set himself on a headfirst expedition. And headfirst stood a large science hall.

He approached the brick building, where he was shortly stopped.

"Hello. Where's the entrance?" asked Andrei.

"Where it says entrance."

"Oh. I actually can't read that far. Bad eyesight. Thank you."

"Woah—hey. You can't go in. The hall is closed for tonight's event," said the stern man, guarding the door.

"I forgot my backpack inside."

"You forgot your backpack in a staff building?"

"My—"

"—thank you."

Dick, thought Andrei.

"Dick," said Andrei.

"Excuse me?"

"You. Are. A. Dick."

The stern man blinked, speechless. He watched Andrei in surprise that a conflict was brought to confrontation. He was not prepared to engage, felt awkward, and sensed in Andrei's eyes that the boy was willing to take things further, but Andrei walked away to the side of the building toward a noise.

Struggling to keep a bloated trash bag upright, a custodian pushed a cart out the door. The door flew open and the custodian approached the dumpsters ahead. Andrei rushed over to the opening and entered inside.

"Shit," he said.

It was a supply room. With nothing in it. No other door. No window. No entry. There was a shelf with cleaning supplies, a few half-stocked janitor carts laying around, an assembly of used rags on a chair, fresh mops leaning in a far corner of the room, an old television, and several pairs of worker boots. Andrei's shoes were starting to smell, so he removed them and scavenged the boots. He threw his old pair in a bucket, dried his legs with fresh towels, and slid his feet inside, pulling the laced tongue until he felt the boots fit, perfectly in fact.

As he looked around. Andrei noticed that behind the metal shelf of supplies was a cream-painted ladder attached to a hatch. Andrei pulled back the shelf and started to climb.

Nearing the top, his heel kicked the shelf and a bottle of cleaning spray dropped to the floor and puddled the ground. His body stuttered. *Should I go back down?* But he thought, *If it's disinfectant, is it really a mess?* Gracing the janitor with his sanitary contribution, Andrei hurried up the ladder, unlocked the hatch and emerged on the roof.

Once standing, he booted the steel opening shut and embraced the rumbling groan of the building's ventilation. Andrei studied the view out below. Students walked in pairs or groups, some napped on grass fields, and about forty younglings on a field trip followed their teacher. Silent scooters were driven in all directions and tree branches swayed to the earth's breath. *So much green,* he thought.

He crossed the rooftop, where the west exterior of the building was built in the shape of a sharp 'U.' There were a set of outdoor stairs attached to the main ground, but it was at least a twenty-foot jump to make it to that platform. Unable to bear that impact, Andrei looked for another way down. The other hatches that led inside were locked. There was no ladder connected to any edge of the rooftop. But as he stepped back out on the edge, he noticed that beneath every window was a fringe of cement, wide enough to hook a pinky finger. *Perhaps we could use these outer sills to reach the staircase.* The windows, however, were too far apart from each other and the distance would prove too challenging for his body to jump from one to the other. Andrei measured that if he could place his foot on one sill, and safely hold himself, he could swing himself to the neighboring plane that cornered the wall he was on, brushing off the plain brick, which would slow his fall to the stairs from a height he could handle.

Carefully, Andrei turned his body, facing the building, and gripping the edge of the rooftop, squeezed his fingers against the concrete like lobster claws, and slowly lowered his body. His feet searched for holding and found the first window fringe, so he let his fingers go and leaned his body against the glass. The white blinds of the office were shut, and Andrei saw the reflection of a sweaty, unrecognizable face of vigor and adrenaline. *Is that me?* he asked. His muscles shrieked for attention and remembering he was hanging off a science wall, he lowered his stance, got on his knees, placed his hands where his feet were, and dangled. Andrei dropped his legs down. Now, it was force he needed.

Hanging, he kicked his knee out to gain momentum, but aired short. On the second sway, he swung himself out to the corner, released, and kicked off the wall. He flew down from the air and plummeted straight toward the staircase. Andrei's shoulders crushed against the steel with a bang that echoed campus. He brought himself to his feet and rubbed the sweat off his hands on his scarf as walked down the stairs, toward home.

Andrei cut through an art exhibit of sculptures until he faced his next hurdle.

In the following building, he saw a ladder, but its mount was locked. *Probably twelve feet in the air,* guessed Andrei. He noted a blue recycling container and rolled it toward the ladder. Closing the lid, he stepped atop the bin and climbed up. Once there, his new view was exquisite—a view of the botanical garden, which felt like an old, familiar lover he once knew intimately.

Andrei stood there for a while. Watching the world from a high ground was like the winter—one gets something back, something that was either lost or taken away. And by indulging from this distance, or surviving the cold season, either that missing thing gets returned, or one's emptiness gets stitched together. Andrei took a new ladder down.

Sometime along the quest, Andrei hiked to the rooftop of a library. In front of a ventilator, he saw undone clothes sprawled across the cement. He approached the quiet moaning and saw two students in the middle of a fuck. They did it standing and faced outwards to the campus. Peeking, he laughed and felt like Mars.

Andrei looked at the students, who were mostly unaroused. He zoomed out again and had that similar perspective he'd had in the café. He called these "terrain thoughts." *Look at what animals we are,* he surveyed. He could not wrap his head around such a beastly activity of muscle tissue.

The two students looked more like wildlife than people. They faced away from each other and their minds, a movie theatre, only played the show of sensations from their sweating organs, in which no story or characters were involved. Watching the woman's head bobble and seeing the athletic boy's hips pound against hers, it seemed like the college boy was gutting a fish with a finger. *From this angle, his penis is just fudging her stomach.* Andrei cringed. And yet, however much it made him want to vomit, Andrei wanted to gut someone like that too. He wanted not just the pleasure of fucking, but the loss of a woman's control.

There was an exclusive euphoria of controlling someone in sex, which shared ties with a kind of godliness. In the workplace, it was uncivil to pull another's hair and call them bad names—*but for some reason,* Andrei thought, *we invite all the unsuppressed actions and ask others to pull the strings of someone's skeleton.* In naughtiness, one felt above humanity, a momentary controller of fate—as if each move of their own body could incite an allowance from another human, who was normally programmed to defend. There was influence. Dancing proved similar—action and reactions of the other. Or perhaps in conversation, when a person played with another's weakness and selected certain sensitive words to provoke them.

The two humans continued to arouse each other's nerve endings, possibly referring to it as love. Andrei wondered which conduct it was—a meaningless transaction or love. He saw the boy fascinated by his own body, staring down in intrigue at its current reality. Then the girl, who closed her eyes, never once engaging the male. Andrei sighed and saw again two fishes wearing human costumes, doing it like dogs. He left for another building.

Two more structures lay ahead. Andrei went up the ladder of a wide establishment with windows as walls and vents powerfully sending the smell of bread and spices which warmed his happy nose. It must have been a dining hall. After the previous scene, he had no appetite. Andrei continued on the roof. It seemed almost empty, and in a way, it completely was. The girl in the corner was not there.

She was so still that Andrei did not notice her until he made his way to leave. Her legs dangled to the reverbed song playing through her wireless earphones—and that was where Alejandra was, on the planet of the second stanza. The song was called 'Runner.' It continued: *The first days are always okay, that's not why I'm afraid. It's the eighth day, in the middle of May, when we look at each other and have nothing more to say.*

Alejandra had been broken up with. She failed to understand why—things had been so exciting to her and in reality, they were. But each walk they went on, the man would mumble a sentence, jokingly—a repetition that Alejandra did not pay much attention to. In her memory, it was vaguely him mentioning a fear of having nothing more to say to his lover. That sometime later, "two people will be in a room together and inevitably expire from each other."

He was in terror of that painful feeling of knowing a bond had reached its end. And when the person he loved was especially magnificent, that unfair feeling was too frustrating of a paradox: an incredible person to talk to, but nothing left to talk about. It made love not worth it. Alejandra's ex-boyfriend could not withstand the tone of voice from a person that tried to search for things to say, politely reviving a mummified connection. To him, this future turned all things brown, so he ran before they spoiled. He made the choice when he and Alejandra were eating lunch and for a brief period, nothing was said. He panicked. "This is it," he said to himself. He knew it would hurt Alejandra. But in his mind, a heart sliced in two was better than the slow ache of starvation.

They met in a mandatory seminar during their freshmen year. He really liked her—especially the way her femininity stimulated him. Alejandra was the type of girl that never let a boy entirely have her. If his lips tried to go for a random peck, she would turn the opposite way and smile a "no." They would be seated at a restaurant and her peppy, shy voice would say, "Thank you for taking me here, but don't expect anything." He felt like he had her slippery heart in his hands, but never held it—instead her heart levitated, floating a few centimeters above his twitching fingertips, shining like a fickle disco ball, magnetized in the air by Alejandra's masterfully crafted tension. She perfected this practice and learned it from her older sister. Except Alejandra felt that she was not as intelligent or gorgeous as other women, and that this prowess was all she had.

Alejandra came across that popular song 'Runner' many years ago, but it had such an upbeat melody that she always danced to it and never bothered with the lyrics. Even if she had, they would not have made sense to her. But now, with the boy's eyes still imprinted wherever she looks, and her hands so freshly left that she could feel his fingers interlaced with hers, Alejandra searched for him in everything. She watched movies where the characters' issues sounded like his. She read passages in English class and thought of the boy, asking, "Is that you?" She found him in this song— realizing she loved a person terribly afraid of inertia. He'd told Alejandra this many times, but his comments had been so small in the grand scheme of things. She now knew that the largest parts of people escaped in tiny ways, tiny words, and tiny looks. One was not permitted to let themselves go and because they gripped so tightly trying to keep together the puppet they presented, parts of identity snuck their way out of holes, and released, transforming into something like a harmless quip their lover would forget. But their lover would remember it. Afterward. The schedule of human understanding was almost always set: afterward.

Andrei watched her repeat the song over and over. Her recital fascinated him. When he felt it was time, he made his way out. But the comet flickered inside his body and he knew what he had to chase. Andrei interrupted.

"What are you listening to?" he shot out.

She did not turn around. *Oh! She can't hear me,* he said to himself.

Then Alejandra picked her nose with her index and wiped the booger on her jeans. *Well, I can't interrupt her now,* he thought. *She'll get embarrassed.* So he stood and waited respectfully for another minute.

Andrei reached out to tap her on the shoulder but did not want to frighten her. She bobbed her head to the song as he backed away and considered another fashion to get her attention. A part of him did not want to disrupt her—she was so with herself that stopping her rhythm would be like interrupting a play or telling a healthy sea animal to stop swimming. But greater than the need to admire was his need to follow that admiration—which meant talking to the stranger.

Andrei undid the laces of his right boot and in her direction, tossed it right off the building. Alejandra's body jolted and she turned around.

"Did you just throw your shoe?"

"I didn't want to creep you out," he said.

"Right. Scaring me is much better."

"You were on your headphones. I just wanted to know what song you were listening to."

"Um…" Alejandra flushed pink. She did not want to tell Andrei the song because she did not want to be read. Either he could assume the song was about her or would discover how desperately she wanted to understand a person she loved. She would not give herself away to just anyone.

"I just threw my shoe."

"Okay, right. It's called 'Runner.'"

"You kept replaying it."

"How long were you standing there?"

"Like, a good stand."

"It's a nice song."

"How nice?"

She held out one of her earbuds and Andrei sat on the edge of the roof with her. They listened. Alejandra was a few inches taller than him and her black denim jacket was blemished with dirt and stains. She would never wash a jacket he wore. She could still smell his cigarettes. Andrei registered her hair smelled bad and guessed she hadn't showered for a few days, but did not make that comment.

The two were silent. The song played. The song ended. The song restarted. Then after some repetitions, they became the song.

Once Alejandra and Andrei regained themselves, he asked her why she replayed it.

"This guy I met. The song is about him."

They listened to it again.

"You know the problem with runners?"

"What?" Alejandra perked up. She wanted to know the problem with runners. It would help her gain a sense of footing, after living in her head all week. She needed to understand him. *What's the problem with runners? Tell me,* she said in her head.

"Had I run away from you, I'd never know this song. The problem with runners is that they lose out on music they need to hear."

"When he's ready..." she broke off. She tucked her lips inside and turned away. "When he's ready, I might already be gone."

"Yeah."

The two silently accepted the damage of a life that promised nothing. There was nothing more that needed to be said. Andrei hugged farewell to Alejandra, who put her earphones back in. She replayed the song—and instead of feeling like there was something left to do, she listened to a song that reminded her of someone she once knew.

With one boot, Andrei descended the ladder. Once he made it down, he wiped the dust from his fingers on his khakis. He looked around and could not find his other shoe.

He searched inside the bushes, every inch of the walkway, and defeated, looked up to Alejandra for help, but she was gone. He did not exactly mind the rough ground, and for the sake of balance and comfort, he removed his other shoe and tossed it in the trash.

Barefoot, he approached one final building before reaching home.

IO

THE HOSPITAL

It was the largest establishment on campus, but in a way, he would soon know, the most empty.

The hospital stood twelve stories high and Andrei came from the east parking garage stairwell to reach the top. Once on the roof, he jogged across and saw his apartment ahead.

He came to a halt.

He looked down and spotted a row of small ceiling windows. These skylights led to a set of rooms that welcomed the sun. This highest floor of the hospital inhabited patients in subacute care. What Andrei saw saddened him so deeply that if one turned to the boy, they would assume he'd knelt on the floor to spy a better view, but it was because he could not stand. He stared below at individual people alone in their rooms who were unable to move and speak. If they did move, they were prompted by involuntary body twitches, such as the neck jolting suddenly to the side, the teeth grinding, or eyelids shuttering at slow speed. The patients were not in comas, but rather suffered from brain injuries—some young persons, some old.

Andrei watched. It made him weak.

Sometimes, Andrei would feel like the moon. When he dined in solitude, when he masturbated to the couple at the hotel, or when he finished a book he could tell no one around him about, he felt singular and unaccompanied, like the stupid, radiating circle stuck in the sky. His soul would glow softly, through the darkness, deadened, but there, as if solemnly leaving a light on for anyone to come join him. Andrei would feel so far away from everyone else, like a floating object in space, lost in orbit, that no hand worried about, remembered, or attempted to retrieve. And looking at this top floor of patients so low, he saw twenty-two moons. The moons were above their beds, in an area of the universe that was so cut off that the world forgot about them, if it even knew they existed. Who has time for those people on floors that have nothing but time? His body felt so connected to the other bodies below, each different, in their own contorted position. He immediately felt a pang of guilt. How could he relate to these people who had it so much worse than him? But his spirit, which for the whole day went forward, understood as clear as day. Pain that hollowed a man, that is completely hollowed, could not be compared or measured. Especially when it came to feeling like the moon, as all could, one need not argue. They knew the feeling or they didn't.

Of the twenty-two windows, Andrei counted twenty of the patients to be unvisited. So he paid his visits to each of them.

And of the two rooms that had visitors, the first was a family. A young man, who Andrei recognized as the son, wore a white baseball cap and red tracksuit. He stood by the bed. Lying down was the father, completely immobile. His skin yellowed like old mustard and his teeth resembled tree bark. The mother was sitting on the chair, going through her bag as if trying to distract herself. The son's mouth moved fast. Andrei watched him berate the mother. Over a matter quite small, he threw his hands up, waving them sharply as he shouted. The mother sat there helpless, ashamed, and defended herself by agreeing. The son assumed a patriarchal position and typically did this when he and his mother were alone. He could stretch himself in anger and his powerless mother could not do anything. The son was at an age when his mind was sharp and his reasoning hot, so he would correct his mother with seemingly intelligent observations while spitting quick, insulting remarks. And like the son who reached that certain age, there came a time in a mother's life when she could not compete with the angry passion of her child. Her strength was beaten, her body slowing, and so entered cold, defenseless years. She surrendered as the son chastised her and she cried about it later—having only the energy to withhold her tears from her unfamiliar baby boy. These sons were all over the world—who used their position to feel something. He thought he was being civil and smart, even impressive, when actually he was nothing but vile. They controlled their female parent, sometimes in public, but worse in private, with nasty attitude and impatience. There is nothing more uncomfortable than a son being cruel to his mother. It is the epitome of unfairness, and rarely did these sons own a mirror that revealed how irrationally brutal their treatment was.

Andrei watched the son retire from the room. The woman closed the door and buried her face in her hands. Her body shook to powerful exhalations and tears, with the might she once had and could only deploy in the dolorous activity of weeping. After some minutes, she ran out of saltwater. Her light makeup was smeared dark. As if turning into the moon herself, the mother looked up to God and saw Andrei watching from above.

She was so sad that her shock did not register. Though frowning, she looked at him.

I cannot do it, stranger, said her green eyes.

Andrei gazed at the mother with pity, and his brown eyes told her that he was sorry, on behalf of sons. And he placed his hand against the glass, whose timing and gesture indicated a further statement after his apology. His palms seemed to perfectly say, *"We do not see it now. But you are the greatest thing about us."*

The mother's sobs restarted but she kept her face angled toward Andrei. She placed her hand over her heart. Andrei wiped the tears from his own eyes, quick and rough, as if to communicate that she needed to stay strong for a while until the monster inside her son died. And she knew it in her heart too that she needed patience, but being alone was so hard and she was too weak. They looked over at her husband who she needed. Though because of Andrei, another woman's son, this mother was not alone. And from his smile, he told her that she could endure through private laughter. *It's all so funny! Look at your makeup, you raccoon.* And the woman smiled too, wiping her eyes. Her life before her husband's work accident was always so lighthearted and it pleased her to return to that lightness. Andrei stood up as the mother did. And walking away, Andrei saw her approach the bedside toward her husband facing the ceiling, who could not move, but was moved—and saw everything.

Andrei walked over to the last window, the final patient with a visitor. The man's injury was severe. His body was stiff and twisted at various angles. His wrists curled themselves into a pale chest that sunk inwards, molding to the bed. His legs bent into themselves, like a fetus, and his ankles slanted to a degree where his worried bone protruded under a layer of thin, stretched skin. He was still. He might have been only a year or two older than Andrei. His jaw was released, and saliva dripped on a towel set prepared beneath his chin. His eyes fixed themselves on the wall.

The woman, who pulled up a chair beside him, rubbing his hands, seemed at first his wife. At least, Andrei thought, his girlfriend. But Andrei could barely see on the side table a photo frame of a young boy and young girl who posed like siblings for a photo: the boy was on his bicycle and the girl ran after him, catching up to pull his hair, laughing, as the boy stuck out his tongue. But on that day, as Andrei saw, the girl was not pulling his hair, but brushing her brother's head gently. And the boy's tongue was not out so as to tease, but hung loose on the side of his mouth without permission. Andrei looked back at the photo. *That's her,* he thought, squinting. *And that's him… before…* he said to himself.

The woman took a deep breath and placed her hands on her brother's thighs. She rubbed his skin. The patient's mouth then opened and closed. Andrei paid such close attention that the slight movement from the brother startled him.

The woman nodded her head, as if to encourage her brother to keep going, wherever he was going. And then over his bedsheet, she rubbed his lower sex organs and massaged them, stimulating his brain in the smallest, noticeable way. Andrei got up to leave—the sight disgusted him. What was he witnessing? She then put on gloves and gripped her brother's insensate penis. Andrei kept watching her, unsure how to describe what he felt, but felt, and was pulled by the weight of something tragic, complicated, and real inside that room. He continued to watch.

The sister stroked the cock of the brain-injured patient and oftentimes, looked away to regain herself as though she was suffocating from tear gas. But over time, she aroused her brother, desperately, carefully, and routinely. In moments, the patient's face would move. Then he would let out a small, quivering smile, and she would continue. Andrei could see that she was heaving with tears, but did not know if they were of sadness or joy. Still, she fought through them. When he finished, she took off her gloves. The sister took hold of her brother's hand and nodded again, saying something. She put her forehead on his and seemed to pray.

Then, she held up a board displaying a palette of colors. Andrei guessed she was trying to teach him words, perhaps to help his vocabulary and memory. But she moved the board in circles, closer then farther from his face, and did not speak at all. This was something different. He watched her further, how she rotated the board in new directions, and soon realized her intention. The sister was merely showing her brother colors. Just colors. That in a room painted white, curtains blue, and hospital gowns polka-dotted white and blue, she could use her visitation to show him the other part of the world cut off from him: light and shade. She presented him with the vigor of red, the funkiness of orange, and the mystery of purple. The brother smiled. Andrei was touched to consider that for the souls in these sensitive rooms, the greatest gift to give was the observation of color.

Andrei could not guess how long the brother had been in this condition. For all he knew, the patient might not have known that smartphones existed, who the president was, or that the pandemic had even occurred. Andrei contemplated the brother's state—and imagined a mind sinking down an infinite well of scattered thoughts and gloom. He speculated the likely craze one would result to from being imprisoned inside a room, isolated from all things and all people for years. The brother had no choice but to stare at the ceiling and listen to a machine that breathed for him. He could not taste the flavor of fruit, of beer, of cheese, or any delight to the tongue. He would not know temperature. He could not scratch himself nor could he ask to be scratched. He must have lost count of the days and not know if it was a Thursday in April or Sunday in May. If a nurse said something to him, he was forfeited the human naturality to respond. If a nurse hurt him, he could not protect himself. He had memories, but no friend to create more with. Andrei assessed him further, finally formulating that this man was deprived of love and touch. He could not hold anybody, nor fuck anybody. The sister's attempt to give him that pleasure, however much she struggled, was a way to free him from that room. She understood that all people wanted to be touched, and as hard as it was to admit, she would too if she were in his place. His sister believed that if she could improve the situation, she would have—but there was only her and his emptiness. And thus, she filled it.

Andrei did not understand what he had seen. And either his unblinking eyes welled up from focusing so carefully below or for another reason. But he chose to swallow the matter in its entirety. If the quick world, worried of itself, saw through the same skylight, a different level of acidity would rain against the glass. Society would spit out and brand her with names and cast the sister out. But Andrei felt her engagement was more fragile and needed time to defend in argument. Time no one would give her. It was a situation sincere hearts find themselves in of raw, dirty discomfort they cannot share. A day-to-day, on-the-ground, actual trouble of skin and reality—like flat tires, psychotic parents, immobilized brothers—a pain that the restless world would have no patience for and so was kept secret in the shadows of tragedy along with lost people, lost things, and real life.

The woman kissed the man's forehead and waved goodbye to her brother. Andrei lifted his hand and waved goodbye for him, and climbing down from the hospital roof, walked gratefully home on his two healthy legs.

II

HOME

The moment Andrei looked up at his apartment, he felt it all over again. The profound irritation with life that he'd lived with for so many years. Nothing could interest his stale pulse. There existed no food, no art, no passion to excite him any longer than an afternoon. There was not a single unit of life in that cold state of richness that could inspire him, especially not his bedroom.

He scanned the stained-glass windows paneling the wide, brick building. Kingship had lost its shine.

Andrei recalled the mornings when he zombie-walked over to the upscale sushi bar down the street. He would wake up and his hair would fly northeast here and southwest there. Andrei would enter the door in his black silk pajamas.

"Good morning, Andrei. Welcome in."

The hostess would make an exception to their closed-toed shoe policy for their local regular and invite Andrei and his gold slippers inside.

Andrei sat there, countless mornings, before he even brushed his teeth. He would stare fixedly at the table, sometimes recalling a dream, sometimes feeling as if he was still in one. The server would come and find that the airy, expected politeness that came in speaking to a waiter had already died in this guest at a different restaurant. Now, when they came to his table, Andrei was calm and would say his order, softly, as if telling a secret to a close friend. No jitters. No recited quips. Andrei asked carefully how their days were and held onto their every word, listening with a reserved, but fierce intensity. The servers respected Andrei—he tipped well and they especially loved that Andrei asked for all of their recommendations. Though inevitably, that side of their relationship dwindled when Andrei had tried more food on the menu than the staff had.

He was also often the only one there. Coming so early, the rest of the world would either be at work or have set their reservations for night. The manager made sure that every morning when they opened shop to prioritize kitchen prep and set his table. Most diners would feel elevated by the sushi bar's deluxe architecture, expensive plates, and ornate tables. Their impressed fingers would lie gently on the counters, as if afraid to break something or snap the stand. But either because Andrei knew the exact weight the table could handle as if it were his own, or merely did not care, he dropped his yawning chin above his crossed arms until his order came. The hostess would peek over and find the sorrowful image of a young man alone eating freshwater eel at nine in the morning. Once in the middle of his meal, after devoting some time to his fish, she would watch the boy sip a hot serving of jasmine green tea with passion, as if there was some trinket in the bottom of the cup that would give him an answer he searched for.

Andrei blinked back to the present and faced his building. It was the soul again, talking. He understood that there was nothing to be gained if bodies returned to yesterday. He knew yesterday—yesterday was all he had. Persistence used to be his goal; perhaps, he once believed, if he endured more days, eventually life would come together, either ultimately or through a single event. Books and art and politics said to keep going. But while persistence was other men's answer, their conflicts were not his. How could a man totally trust history's advice when today, the sparrow breaks its old route and flies over that jacaranda tree and not the usual? Persistence was not Andrei's answer. He needed deviation.

He heard Mars' voice and remembered her tired hands. *There is chance in different routes,* he thought. So he turned away from home and walked to the cinema.

12

THE CINEMA

He went down Gayley Avenue, obeying its curves and length.

The rough sidewalk was accented with a skateboarder's worst nightmare: cracks and molten concrete that rose a few inches off the ground. Beer cans from the row of frat houses flattened on the curb. Blue gum. Fresh leaves. The road, however, was impeccable. It was, after all, Beverly Hills and if one turned their neck north, the estates of Bel Air stood high and mighty.

After Gayley's crooked, playful charm, Andrei turned left to Broxton Avenue. Broxton was where the cafés were, the ice cream shops, and the oily bites. The sidewalk was not so congested. Most of its recurring pedestrians were in class during the afternoon. At that moment, there were families, medical staff on their lunch hour, and the homeless. This was the village.

A rush of music boomed to the side of Andrei. His body flinched. It played so loudly and everyone around covered their ears. Andrei's skin flushed red because his startled reaction made him upset. He looked toward the muscle car with peppery eyes. The driver, rapping along to the song, and revving his engine, did not notice a man at his window, until

Andrei knocked on the glass. The man jolted in the driver's seat and looked at the stranger pounding on his window. Andrei frowned at the driver, asking in his challenging eyes why the music was being played so loudly. Andrei did not gesture or instruct the driver to lower the volume, but simply wanted to talk. A clash would have taken place, if not for the fire in Andrei's eyes that scared off the driver. The car drove away, unsure of itself. Andrei looked down, surprised he was standing on the street. He was aware he approached a car, but time seemed to run in a linear, silver sprint that completely escaped from his recollection. Andrei walked on.

The driver, now hundreds of feet away, had been in a trance. And Andrei had broken it. Suddenly, the driver's thoughts swirled loud enough to be heard under the music: *Who was that? Why the fuck was he staring at me? Man, I hate that guy. I HATE him. I would drive back right now and beat his ass. But would I win… I think so…. I think I would… I'm not that strong… I've never been that strong. I should take up boxing like Aaron… Then I can beat his ass… If I was strong, I'd hurt everyone. Why am I so angry? Why didn't I do anything then? I'm so weak… Why do I want to hurt people?* The driver pictured the bigger men who once hurt him, the reason for much of his anger. Understanding oneself was simple because pain was exact and clear. The issue was in the avoidance—and the driver was running from himself.

In fairness, all drivers on the road ran the same afraid way in some capacity. But he played music so loudly he could not hear his pain. He stunted his growth beneath a bass that decorated his aura and lyrics that hardened the glass parts of him. He was indeed an autumn leaf dipped in concrete. He wanted sound, any sound but his own thoughts. Ears that needed songs louder than the mind were ears afraid of what they might hear inside. Then, like a phantom, his bullies reappeared to tell him the truth, but he turned his music up further and sang to a song that was not his.

Andrei continued on Broxton Avenue. There were skilled promoters who sent compliments to passersby, fishing for a participant's signature or donation. There were clothing stores, banks, and cuisines. Andrei saw a poet selling chapbooks at a bookstand. The sign, a little tacky, if not charming, read: *Books & Chocolate*.

"Hey, help yourself to some chocolate," the poet said to Andrei.

Andrei nodded, went over to the stand, and unwrapped some candy from the bowl. To his right, a young woman inquired about the book the poet was selling.

"So what's your book about?" she asked.

"Oh, of course. Er—it's like…" said the poet. "Well, it's hard because there are thirty different poems, and they're each about different things."

"Wow, that's cool! And what are they about?"

The poet struggled. Andrei looked over to the bead of sweat beginning to roll down the writer's forehead. It seemed the author wanted to talk, but felt humiliated he could not produce words at the moment.

"They're about… the book covers—kind of… life. Life and people."

"That's so nice! I'll check it out sometime. Thanks for the chocolate," said the customer.

"Have a great day," mumbled the poet. She left and he turned to Andrei. "Let me know if you have any questions."

Andrei flipped open to page twenty-seven of the book. The poem was called 'Break Room.' And the poet wrote:

> I limp inside the break room,
> Not because I've a bad leg,
> But because sometimes when I limp,
> It makes more sense to be alive.
> I could not locate sense outside.
> And I slump my body on this shit couch,
> Dirty hands from cleaning, eyes sore
> Until I play a song and stare at the wall.
> The song is about lonely nights in New York—
> And I feel far away and say: "Ah, it can be this."
> I love these minutes, these cold few,

Because it is okay to be the color blue.
We're not all sunflowers here, I cannot yellow.
I prefer to sit here with my curled leg,
Listening not to laughter or information, but voice.

The anxious poet from behind the booth eyed Andrei, trying to see what page he was on. But the book was held slanted, so the poet could never tell. Andrei looked the page over and, recalling the woman's question from earlier, realized the writer's difficulty.

There was no plot. The book was not about friendship or love—but about lines like "when I limp, it makes more sense." To Andrei, the poem held itself there, about someone escaping from loud rooms, and workplaces, to somewhere real. And he played some music that reminded him of what life could be.

"Ah, it can be this," read Andrei. *Yes.* Andrei smiled to himself. *It can be.*

But, whatever that was, it did not make a good selling point. The crux of the chapbook could not exactly be pitched. If the poet replied to the inquiring woman, "It's partly about curling your leg," she would walk away disinterested, and potentially uneasy. *But that is what it's about,* thought Andrei. *This poet's book is about his lines—specific lines of an image of a work room, a thought that occurs, a secret like a New York song, or an inability to be a sunflower.* And page eighteen was some point about pillbugs. The effort of the collection could not be bundled, summarized, or grouped. None of these subjects would make it to a billboard. It could not be advertised. There was nothing immediately captivating about humanity, which could not be understood without first being read. But those little ideas, little words, and little lines were why the writer would die for his writing. Perhaps what could be advertised so successfully was not worth dying for.

"How much for the book?" asked Andrei.

"Ten dollars," replied the poet.

"It's hard to promote. I think they just have to open it up and read it."

"I should write things that are easier to say out loud," laughed the poet.

"I'll buy two copies if you promise not to," he said.

He placed a bill behind the bowl of chocolate. The writer thanked Andrei with a nod, more for his comment than the purchase. And with that, Andrei walked away with two copies.

Andrei recognized the sleeping man on the pavement. When he was normally awake, he dragged his feet around the village and searched the trash bins. His bowl-cut hair was smoky and stuck out like a porcupine. He never made a sound. The dirt under his fingernails was as brown as the baggy blazer he wore, though his slacks were darker, much like the smears of charcoal around his blue eyes. Andrei placed one of the copies beneath the head of that old man, whose dream was redirected to a happier place from the paper pillow gifted to him.

The movie theatre towered straight ahead. The classic Spanish building was crisp and armed with the style of golden age Hollywood. It was tiered like a wedding cake and a large marquee of showtimes displayed electric in blue and red. Behind it were linen-colored stones engraved with pointed arches and elaborate tracery.

It only had a single auditorium, so one movie was shown a day. Andrei ordered his matinee ticket, a small popcorn that resisted a seventy-five-cent upgrade to a medium, and a bottled soda pop. It was him in the theatre and a couple making out in the back. They even brought a blanket. Andrei looked over at them and thought there was no way he could do what they did. Love. *I'm too lonely to know what love is. I would go around calling this love and that love.* With that, the movie began.

It was indie and nice. The film followed a young girl growing up. The audience watched her go from a happy child slipping down the slide at the park to a businesswoman rising in the company. We see her opening scenes of youth—revealing that nothing was as dramatic as when a person was young. The slug on the ground became a part of their story, their fun little feet could skip, and they could get away with sentences like: *"You have a big nose, but you're funny and I really like you! Do you want to play with me?"* And the children shared their blood and acceptably kissed each other's wounds. When it was time to say goodbye, they ran up to hug each other. Everything was news to their ears and they reacted with a freshness adults cannot help but envy.

Then the movie tracked the child to later. Keep in mind, that nothing in that human being had changed, except for their body growing and having to say "yes" two to three hundred thousand times in the direction the world asked them to take. She was much older and her park dates had changed to dinners and her playful hugs changed to firm handshakes and new friends to potential networking opportunities. She did not speak her mind, but now played conversational games of power—mirroring, concealing, and manipulation. *The animal part of humanity fades over time*, seemed to say the movie, and indeed it was very sad to watch people shrink.

The story was okay, but the acting bothered Andrei. Sometimes he would watch a scene and then it would go to the next; Andrei would blink, bewildered at the time that had passed. The film just went by. Scenes would jump to the next but his mind was the same. *Why?* He noticed that the lead actress in her later years was extremely gorgeous, except some sharp concentration in him blocked out her beauty. This seated heart screamed for the movie to shatter him. And it drew upon him that this was another film that the world was not bothered by of its acting. In fact, they did not even see it. In its short scenes, audiences were hypnotized for an average of five to eight seconds by an actor's beauty and if the editor timed it right, and with enough spectacle, movies could get away with doing nothing. Gorgeousness stimulated the mind. "Wow, they are so beautiful," the audience was forced to think—and then by jumping to the next beautiful part fast enough there was something called a movie. And the movie seemed to use the actors' appearances to drive most of the scenes. And many actors in different scenes sort of just stood there, handsome, and whispering. That was their strategy—mumbling murmurs of breath and rasp. Their indecisive bodies were unnaturally still, as though they had close-ups when the shot was wide. All of the actors' voices were dumbly lowered to a safe natural cadence while in an unnatural situation and yet seeming real, no actual thought needed to be shown. *Beauty is good,* says the industry. *Sell that. Sell beauty! Make it beautiful. Ugly stories about beautiful people. It naturally turns a crap film into a decent one. The people are left with a good impression, as though having watched something fascinating. Make sure to let the camera sit on those beautiful people and their faces will give the audience something impossible to understand and give us runtime while they gaze. But having ugly people in it, people that look like people, actors that look like their audience—er, that's not so profound,* says the industry. It was why the scenes moved without Andrei knowing: nothing was done by its actors.

But past that, Andrei was still moved. He talked to the writer in his head:

"The movie, or rather the script, seemed to ask for the earlier *us*—which is not a child, but the suppressed spirit that is born free and deserves to die free."

And it seemed fitting both for Andrei, and hypothetically the creators of the story, that when he got up to leave in the middle of it, he did so as an ode to the film. A statement of departure that said: *If you made the movie for the reason I think you did, perhaps you wouldn't be offended that I left the damn place and decided to chase after life. Inspiration is unlimited, but time is not. Thank you. Goodbye!* He left the poet's book in the seat beside him, took his popcorn and soda, and exited the cinema the way the writers would have wanted.

He left for the cemetery.

13

THE CEMETERY

The place called to him. It was one of those areas by one's home they always drove past and knew was there, but never took the time to visit.

The Westwood cemetery was a large, beautiful field that seemed too green for what it was, to hold what it held. In the daytime, one could almost place a group of children and a ball in any spot on the land and it would have been completely natural to watch them play. The gravestones would merely be fun boards to hit, the rectangular space underneath the benches as goals, and the rotting bodies underneath would simply be some fertilizer that helped the grass feel so fresh.

But it was not until Andrei read the inscriptions on the headstones that it began to feel like the place it was—a park for the nonexistent. And there were so many people who could no longer play. There were more dead than alive if one thought about it. He imagined all the love stories. The years of peace and years of war. The cannon and the guillotine. The babies left in carriages and the miscarriages. The accidental deaths and planned murders. The too early's. The too good's. And the empty grass space designated for the next.

Flowers were placed erectly in front of the tombstones, but sometimes the dedicated names did not match. The

131

bouquet would have *For Tristan* signed on a tag, while the tombstone was inscribed, *Maggie Monelli.* Andrei figured people stole flowers they found above a stranger's grave and brought them to their own loved ones. *Such love,* he thought.

Andrei rested on a bench directly in front of a grave that belonged to: *A father, hard worker, and beloved friend.* He leaned back, resting there, and with each second, his desire to know more about this man grew. *Yeah, he's a father, hard worker, and beloved friend. Weren't we all at some point? What's his kink? The worst thing he's done to a person? The greatest thing he's good at?* That's what Andrei wanted to know. Not titles the man himself would disapprove of. What good was a proper impression in a cemetery filled with thousands of proper impressions? One must be indecent. So Andrei closed his eyes and imagined the father who worked hard and was a beloved friend. Maybe his kink was that he needed to do it in public—in the restroom after a date or at church during mass. Maybe the worst thing he had ever done was work so hard for his family that he never once saw them. Maybe the best thing he was good at was giving gifts to his friends. *Yes, that's it.* He never gave money or handed them gift cards, but instead gave his brothers exactly what filled them the most. One year, he gave a notebook to his buddy John with the same line written over and over in painful cursive. The line said: "Happy Birthday, you get thirteen hours of my life" and repeated until you could see the traces of hand cramps squiggling for life on the forty-second page. *What a good man,* imagined Andrei. *Hell of a mate.*

"Did you know my dad?" a voice said.

Andrei opened his eyes and turned to find a young man, roughly his age, wearing a hood and holding some cheap flowers.

"No, I was just looking. Seemed like a good guy."

"Oh. He overdosed on meth a few years ago. Left me and my twin sister when we were three."

"I'm sorry to hear that," said Andrei, confused. "But you still come?"

"Yeah. I stop by his grave whenever I need a place to pee."

"Shit. The flowers?"

"Oh. These are for Marilyn Monroe," said the son.

"She's buried here?"

"Yeah, you wanna go see?"

Andrei smiled.

"Yeah. That'd be great."

Andrei walked on. "I was sitting there imagining the life your father must have had. Had I known—" he stopped. Andrei looked to his right and the boy was gone. He was not beside him. Andrei glanced back to the grave where they had met and saw the son standing on the bench and taking a long piss. *Ah, right.* The boy who carried flowers waved to Andrei.

The two reached Marilyn Monroe's tombstone and stared in silence at her crypt. The boys sat on the floor of the corridor. It was unreal seeing the name Marilyn Monroe on a dead stone. The memory of her moving body did not make sense unalive. She was too great a force and Death must now be obese. Her crypt was the color of sand and kissed with cherry lipstick all over. Just then a white butterfly landed on the corner of her stone. A realization clicked inside Andrei the moment the butterfly settled itself. He saw, as clearly as a prophecy, the difference between life and death.

There, in front, was a piece of stone that had inscriptions on it. The stone never moved. It did not breathe. It did not love. Inside it was a coffin made of wood that was still. The coffin did not love either. Nor the wood. The body of Monroe was bones—a skeleton that could not know itself. And suddenly there was a butterfly—one that twitched and fluttered. This living organism breathed, could roam around the world, see and be seen, and make any mess it wanted. And here Andrei was, pulsing in a field with another pulse. Andrei could lift his hand and smack the stranger across the face or lean in to kiss him. The rocks could not punish nor kiss. Only life could do that. And life was in Andrei, and the young stranger, too. How miraculous that for a short period, the two of them could focus their eyes, turn their heads, lift their limbs, and run straight into the arms of another person. The living were not rocks or wood, incapable of being affected by chance, but rather forces of momentary magic that could digress and collide with anything it chose. Should a human ever feel bored lying atop their bed, they could change reality and within thirty seconds walk outside and strike up a new conversation with another pulse on the street. The living sound an ancient, sacred, temporary hum that is exclusive to them. Once gone, it can never be retrieved. But if there still, it could do anything. Life became so powerful when one compared the dead to the living. The butterfly glowed angelically to Andrei, who thanked it for its arrival from his beating heart that would miss beating.

Sometimes, a feeling would creep over Andrei. And actually, it would creep over the dead man's son beside him, too. A particular awareness would swallow them both individually, in different moments in their lives, for a few seconds. They would lie in bed and out of nowhere, freeze as they remembered that all sensation would end. Everything they'd worked on would be entirely erased. Movement would cease. The visor of consciousness would be taken off. Andrei, and his new friend, would someday no longer have the capacity to try. And they would no longer remember that they could try. They would simply no longer remember. Death was metal and wood and rock. Life had wings.

"So," said Andrei, finally noticing the son's arm cast. "How'd you get *that* thing?"

"The cast?" said the son.

Andrei nodded.

"Uh, milk."

"What?"

"Yeah."

"Your arm broke because of milk."

"Yeah. I really shouldn't say."

"Do say."

134

"Well, I drank a carton of milk, and I guess it went bad. Real bad. Like my stomach started acting up, and then my roommate said I was convulsing on the floor. I don't remember any of it. But he took me to the hospital. And the next morning, I started to get warts on my arm. Then it became really weak. So weak that when the nurse rolled me out of my room for an X-ray, she knocked my arm out the door, and it broke. But now the skin is calming down and my bones are healing."

"That's wild."

"Weird, right?"

"Milk," said Andrei, stunned.

"And the carton said, 'Great for your bones.'"

"Did you try to sue the company?"

"No, I quite like their milk."

"*Honey Farms?*"

"Yeah."

The boys remembered the taste with pleasure.

"Well, I wish you a safe recovery. How long until it heals?"

"Two months."

"Christ. Well I don't know much about bones, but did the hospital suggest how to speed up the process?"

"They gave me more milk."

Andrei smiled and took a good look at the son. He was baby-faced with a soft, pearl complexion that resembled morning grog that never left and never hardened. He had large, amber eyes. He wore a gray beanie, gray jeans, and the same-colored windbreaker—everything was gray. Andrei did not like the color gray—he felt it was one of those colors that were just handed to people and that one must break away from and say, "No. I'll choose something for myself, thank you." But the gray seemed to fit the stranger.

"What's your name?" asked Andrei.

"Raphael. You?"

"My name's Andrei."

"_____," said the tombstone.

"Bzoozzzzz," said the butterfly.

The metal and rock and wood could not hear from down there. But they would have said, "   ."

There was a quietness to Raphael. Andrei liked that quality in him but found it mistrustful in some moments. The fire in Andrei let itself out:

"Why are you so internal? I see you're about to say something, but then you don't," said Andrei. He had never addressed someone so directly before.

"Um, I used to worry about that. But no one cares what I say or don't say. So I don't say," said Raphael, who had never *been* addressed by someone so directly before.

People had tried to reel Raphael in from his silence. Their attempts were precisely why he felt so uncomfortable. He did not want to be saved or included. He liked to listen. When he asked a question, it was because he wanted to know the answer. But then they turned it around to ask, "What about you?" and this bothered Raphael, who believed the speaker only returned the question out of manners and so was never a real inquiry. Raphael would be pressured to respond and endure the painful seconds of saying something someone did not want to hear. He would trace their faltering eyes, then his words would crumble into sand, and his listener would never notice because they were not interested in the first place.

On another note, Raphael simply hated sentences that began with, "I." He was aware of the sound and effect "I" created—the turning away of chins or an opinion forming in the listener's head presuming narcissism. His avoidance of it was so severe to Raphael that if he wanted to say, "I am thirsty," he would instead say, "Let's grab a drink." "I need help," became "Help!" and "I hate my dad," became "There's hatred stored in me for my dad."

Andrei looked at Raphael, searching for something in him. And a few seconds passed and he drew out of Raphael a man who did not totally believe himself. When Raphael felt this intrusion, he came to his own defense.

"No one cares about anyone else's life, but their own, bro. That's the thing. We're just selfish."

"Some surprise us though. Those unique ones who interest us—they do something new with their body. They mean words differently. They bring us in. The people who amaze us are how we know that the selfishness inside us all along was never selfishness. We were only far from certain people."

"Well. I'm quiet. I don't know if I made myself to be or if that's who I am. But I'm quiet sometimes."

And for a while, they were quiet together. Raphael sat on the grass, pulling strands out of the soil contemplatively, as if his body was moved by the brain's song that said: "Looking… searching… where is it? What is it?" He continued to unearth the field, while Andrei paced around, his legs moving, as if his body, too, was listening to his brain's song that sang: "Something there… ahead… keep going… is it there?"

"I'm leaving Los Angeles," announced Raphael.

"Why are you leaving Los Angeles?" asked Andrei.

"Something about the city. People don't want to see each other. Everything's too far away. A bunch of reasons. On sidewalks everyone avoids each other; it's weird to go up to someone. Most of all, the weather's a lie. Too much sun, and then everyone acts like the sun. You know what I mean? There's so much to do, but no one to do it with."

Andrei sensed that Raphael was going to continue with some larger dialogue, so he laid down on the grass a few feet beside him, bathing in the rare overcast.

"Would you date a woman who sells herself on the internet?" asked Raphael.

"It depends, I suppose, how she sells herself."

"Say that she sends pictures and videos of any part of her body to men who pay. Sometimes she talks to them. A bunch of girls do it. Well, it seems like everyone does it. You go on the site and just see pages and pages of women employed there. So many. It's like the odds of you walking past someone and their naked body being some place on the internet are pretty high."

"Are you trying to pursue one of the girls you met online?"

"I am trying to leave one. After I found out that she's online."

"Oh. I'm sorry, Raphael," said Andrei.

"No, bro, I don't mean to pour my shit onto you. I'm not trying to do that. I have a therapist, but I wanted to ask you genuinely what you think."

"Okay," he agreed. "So you dated this girl. You found out that she does like solo porn and broke up with her," Andrei said, facing the sky. "And by the way, you can pour out your shit. That's sort of why I came to the cemetery. For something like that. Some kind of—actual thing, you know. Yeah."

"Yeah. Alright."

"So go on."

Raphael went on to explain to Andrei that the day he caught her, she confused his own reaction. His girlfriend told him that she had every right to do what she wanted with her body. The work she did was her own and that was private. She added that plenty of guys would even feel turned on to have a girlfriend like her. "Babe, they have to pay and you get me for free. I'm all yours," she said. And she calmed him down and he felt calm. He apologized and was disgusted by his outburst. *She was right*, he repeated to himself. Raphael told Andrei that he felt like a monster. That perhaps Raphael was wrongly tyrannizing her freedom through some primitive possessiveness. But weeks went on and a voice in his heart began to cry. Then it cried to her.

"Babe, you're not all mine," said his crying heart. "And I can't explain it—this feeling in me that hates what you do. But it feels wrong. For some reason, it feels wrong. If it was right, why'd you keep it from me?"

"You're trying to control me. This is a double standard. You're doing a man thing where you can't help your own dick. Be open-minded, Rafa. This is my work and it's how I pay rent," she fired at him.

"Look… No… I'm not sure… Okay, there's something inside me like a polygraph. I've had this system since I was a kid. If I look at someone who I don't know and I say, 'I love you,' the polygraph in my body rings false and I hear it. When I say, 'I love what life is,' it rings true and I hear that, too. But when I say to it, 'What she does is okay,' it beeps and beeps and it's still beeping—I can hear it—"

"—Raphael, do you not see how that's your problem—"

"—You're profiting off something so dark. Yes, there's a demographic of men who want to pay for it, but not everything we want is good. And I'm sure you don't want to do it—but you do it because it's there."

"Stop. STOP!"

"Okay!" his heart cried.

"What I do has nothing to do with us. I'm not sleeping with any other person, so it doesn't matter. I don't love them, I pretend to love them. I send them photos, I text them, that's it. Do you get it? I shouldn't even need to justify myself…"

"I know, I get it, but it's so hard to explain why…"

"You can't explain it because there's no reason. I'm right, okay? There's nothing else."

Andrei listened to Raphael's recollections.

"I was so fragmented then, but now," he told Andrei, "I can explain it better. But first, do you get me and everything so far?"

"Yes, I understand."

"Okay."

Raphael took a moment. Andrei waited until he was ready.

"She gives herself away, parts of her body, and then shares them with me. This in itself is okay because we all have ex-lovers. My parts belonged to someone else at another time, hers too, yours too, so we can't ever belong to someone fully. The issue seems to be that when we do it, her and I, there's no one inside. She lost herself somehow. I don't know how—in the pretending, in the dark world the internet is, whatever."

"From my understanding, this is a matter of value?" asked Andrei. "Like other men have had her leg, so her leg doesn't mean anything to you anymore?"

"No… no, that's not even it. It's that you can't pretend to give someone your leg. Even if it's just a photo. Legs can't pretend. You can, but legs can't. And when someone gets your leg, it's given. And you multiply that by a hundred, but she has only two. Two little legs. And it's as if her legs know. The body is not meant to be mass distributed, Andrei. We're not large gods in Olympus—we need assistance climbing up the stairs and eventually porcelain teeth to chew our food. Thousands of strangers have every part of my girlfriend's body, down to the ears. But the one thing they don't have is a woman in the other room sending herself away. They don't have that," said Raphael. "I have that."

Andrei looked at the young man who wore gray, who showered, upon the grass, slow sprinkles from his eyes.

"She will vouch for her freedom," said Andrei. "It's a powerful argument."

"People can do what they want. But if she wants love, she has to be there. I can't marry a mannequin."

Andrei calculated the silence that ensued and the logic of Raphael bringing up this story. He pieced together Raphael's arc.

"So you're leaving Los Angeles?"

Raphael, a little surprised, nodded.

"To run from her?"

"Not just her. Everyone here. My girlfriend's fan base is promoted to audiences only in this city. A kink for locals. A kind of LA category targeting certain women. People get off on that. Tens of thousands of people get off on that. And when I walk around and see another man, I don't trust their shirt and pants. All I see is someone logging onto their computer, paying for another person's feet. And I hate them.

They'll never know soul. Even seeing you, I eyed you and almost vomited."

"I have that effect."

Raphael laughed. And then his laughter grew so hard and perfect, he wept. He wept for having doubted his confusion, for losing his girlfriend, and the desperation to escape Los Angeles. Andrei reached over and held his hand.

Men did not hold each other's hands. It was not a common way of consoling a fellow brother and so both of their stasis broke from the contact. But they kept. And they did not seem to be men in those minutes who hated hairy, veiny hands on their own hairy, veiny hands. They seemed other. The grass field, the tears, and the butterfly—these things turned two men into children on an eternal recess with no supervision, or cruel strangers, and an entire earth before them. And they held each other tightly.

"If you want another person to go places with you, this is me," said Andrei, encapsulating friendship in a single offer. "Do you have to leave?"

"I have to go soon, Andrei. Now. I can't... stop... throwing up," cried Raphael.

"Take this," said Andrei. The two sat up. And he removed the stone bracelet on his left wrist and held it out in his palm toward Raphael.

"It's malachite and black something," said Andrei. "I forgot the name of it. But it's for emotional balance and new beginnings. It will be good for travel."

"You believe in this shit?"

"Yes. All of us will. We'll need to."

"Thank you," said Raphael. He took Andrei's gift, conformed his fingers through the bracelet, and rolled it onto his wrist, which instantly felt better.

"Just make sure you charge it. Once a month. Put it under the moon, when the moon is full. You can... lay it on your windowsill or something," said Andrei.

Raphael brushed the new stones on his body. Immediately, he felt protected. A wave of needles struck his heart and brightened his insides. It was not a perfect yellow. He brightened with the butterscotch shade of autumn, which warmed him not to the elevation of joy, but solace of friendship.

The two little boys stayed soft on the field for a few more moments. Once his puffy eyes recovered, they embraced with a goodbye once Raphael agreed to start heading out of the city. Andrei wished him well and Raphael did the same. Andrei, having been on the outskirts himself, would have normally been destroyed by this goodbye. Raphael was the kind of friend that would make a day worthwhile. But as Andrei walked out of the cemetery, having done all the things he'd done that day, and receiving the exposure to a new way of life, Andrei was not sad. Rather, Andrei felt that this day with Raphael, while short-lived, was the equivalent of being Raphael's friend for many, many years.

Nothing could, of course, replace time devoted to another. They would have enjoyed drinking in the desert, taking a road trip to Arizona, a good street fight or two—though this required time which they did not have. But in an immeasurable sense, one true conversation and a friendship were the same. The heart asked its only ever test: *Did you give me away? Ah, good.* The correspondence of souls begged for existence and never for "longer."

Raphael's departure did not depress Andrei, but immortally fed him. He may not have Raphael to speak with, and Raphael may not have Andrei to sit down and talk to, but they had *spoken*. Given. Lagers in the desert, the fantasy of an Arizona escapade, and bar brawls were already offered between their looks, heart allowance, and exchange of truth. Certainly, one wants those years, but they don't need them. That's the beauty of the real. There was no such thing as "enough" of someone or "more" or "less"—there were only happenings.

And having happened, Andrei left a great, old friend with a new smile.

14

THE UNIVERSITY

Andrei re-entered campus. He walked through busy paths of gleeful clubs waving flyers for their next fundraiser. He passed bulky athletes in hoodies riding their scooters toward the field. Students rested in hammocks on a large, happy hill, where couples lay on the grass, reading, kissing, or playing on their phones. The walkers around Andrei either talked about mid-terms, new matches from dating apps, or which house parties to attend that weekend.

The general noise around him immediately exhausted Andrei, so he walked with his shoulders yanked slightly up, mentally blocking sound from entering his head. Then, making his way to a large lecture hall, he felt like coming closer and so broke into a sprint toward the building and avoided the noise altogether. A group of associate professors walking beside him gasped at Andrei's sudden change of speed. Others gave him strange looks and thought he was in an emergency or plain weird. But Andrei no longer minded. He could not mind. He felt it then and there. In fact, many people would indeed sprint to their destinations, had they no mind.

Once he reached the staircase, he caught air and adjusted his sweaty dress shirt. Andrei continued inside, where cold gusts of air conditioning plastered onto his exhilarated body like thin sheets of ice.

He peered down the hall. It was the time in the afternoon when nearly all rooms were occupied by lectures. Poking his nose at the square glass on each door, he glimpsed scholars taking their exams, students diligently making notes, and discussion groups in heated debate. It appeared a normal school day. But Andrei never had been interested in normality.

Normality seemed suspicious to him. He avoided smart routes, healthy decisions, and standard trajectories, a characteristic born from his years of champagne and luxury. Take talk for example. *What's the pattern?* he thought. To find common interest, a hook usually established good conversation, but never good feeling. Perhaps the hook was a reiteration of a belief general enough to be agreeable, but never to advance a relationship. Maybe it was an evil topic that served mutual negative energy—but once again, no advancement. Instead, Andrei fancied the forsaken, the dreadful, the dusty. He intentionally said yes to what other people said no to. *There must be something worthwhile,* he always thought, *in the apparently worthless, seemingly dangerous, and painfully obvious.* And so after considering the classrooms, Andrei went inside the lecture hall that featured the most bored students.

The professor stood before her sleepy pupils, who all either etched mindless graphite scribbles on college-ruled paper, scrolled through their smartphones with no discretion or stared directly at the teacher whilst planning what they would do after class. They did intend to be disrespectful to their professor. The issue was self-imposed imprisonment. The students were trapped by lofty words first introduced to them in high school and feeling as if they grasped the world enough, had stopped there. Vocabulary like, "existentialism," or the identification of devices like "alliteration" had impressed and froze their roused minds. Though it was better to be trapped by big thoughts than big words; the terminologies learned in high school killed the most learners.

No one turned to look at Andrei entering the room. Perhaps it was natural for students to enter and exit for supposed bathroom purposes. One student had even got away with walking two miles back to his dormitory, making himself breakfast, and leisurely returning to the middle of the lecture. He burped as he passed the barefoot auditor who had entered and taken the front corner seat.

"And this is a character who chooses people. The heroine draws closer to *people*. Does anyone else find that strange?" Her eyes glittered. She was one of those cute types of ladies who pack their own lunch for work. Her homemade salad and portable utensils were in an insulated bag inside her rolling cart.

The class was silent.

Andrei felt sorry for the professor. Though his sympathy did not stem from her lack of being received, but from her appearance, which evidently made reception in her life hard to attain. She was a tall lady with unpleasant features—a large mouth containing teeth that poked her lips forward. Her thick-framed, stylish glasses were an attempt to distract from her awkward face, but only accentuated it. And if one listened to her voice, it was the kind of high pitch sound the ears tuned out naturally. Andrei looked at her eyes, which scanned her notes calmly then back up from her notepad to her students when the thought was ready. And she sometimes resembled a kind of purely excited monkey that loved this part of the day. But it was, as Andrei noticed, simply too hard to appreciate her passion and listen intently beneath the exterior she was born with.

"Sometimes," Dr. O'Hare continued on her own, "sometimes, well, if I need to see something for the first time, I need to zoom out. So I imagine our time here on earth and see little ants!" She laughed to herself and adjusted the frame of her glasses. Andrei grinned at her peculiarities. Then he blinked and remembered he held a similar perspective to her current lesson. *My terrain thoughts,* he said to himself.

"Now, imagine we're all ants. Eight billion ants on a planet! My, that's a lot of ants! Hehe, okay now—if you are looking at a satellite, watching these ants live their lives, I want you to re-evaluate their decisions. Does the ant kick a tiny leather ball really well? Those are soccer players. Does the ant walk over in the middle of the day to help seal the wounds of other ants? Those are doctors. Does the ant like to gather greens in a space and water them? Those are gardeners. Does the little ant ask someone to hold a tiny camera to record them saying made-up sentences to other ants? Those are actors. Everything in this vision seems so lame and puny, right? But those ants are us. And the way we spend our time would look the same as the ants would. There is no difference. That's us! So in our reading, we have a character in a futuristic world who spends their time basically going toward other ants. *Why?*"

Andrei looked back and detected no movement. Then a hand in the back shot up, and Andrei's ears re-focused sharply, but the arm belonged to a distracted student merely attempting to catch a passing fly in the air. Andrei sighed.

Dr. O'Hare quickly eyed Andrei. She saw his feet and said to herself, *These students have all the nerve, don't they.* She took a breath, returned to her notes, and continued:

"Our circumstance at birth is that we are placed on a planet with no prior choice and appointed sensation and awareness—and then nothing after it. There won't be an opportunity to look back or to be ashamed. What to do? Walk the rock and see more of the earth? Fill our playtime with the current inventions? This heroine goes toward *other ants.* Other moving ants. And I keep going back and re-reading the last few chapters and so far I think it's because she agrees with the notion of time and ants. No technology or machine in the world could match the pricelessness of human life—or ant life. It's universally precious. It can't be replicated—so her inclination toward other ants gives her the most value.

Dr. O'Hare scratched her nose, not because there was an itch, but so that while she paused, perhaps a student wished to jump in. Her hope was not met and so continued:

"Nothing else will give her that... kick! She even weeps when she enters rooms sometimes because she gets so overwhelmed by the mercurial chances and pulsing vitality of being in a place with other alive, breathing ants. If she steps on the toe of another ant, they would yell, 'Ow!' and the concept of effect was unbelievably dear to her. Our hearts right now beat as I speak—and I'm so happy to be here with you all, too—but okay, back to this. Oh, wait no. That's all. She finds other ants. It was better to her than anything else on her planet. Diamonds get value from their mining. Gold is a rare metal. People don't have forever. But people also kill and hurt. So we are all simultaneously the worst and best thing for each other."

Andrei smiled, then shifted his legs embarrassingly. He did not have a hard-on, but experienced an uncommon episode in his scrotum. His balls tickled in a prickly wave of zing as he listened to her lecture. It usually happened when he was surprised by some magnificent thing.

"Now does anyone have any questions? Oh, yes! Right there!" said Dr. O'Hare, choosing a student in the middle.

"When logging onto *Vboard,* I couldn't see the dates for our mid-term. The website said... one second, I have it pulled up here... Okay, 'Error 34A, page not found, please contact professor or administrator.' Do you know if there's a problem with the site or something? I just wanted to prepare in advance!" said the student.

"Oh, um, yes. I can go ahead and speak to IT about this," said Professor O'Hare. "Anybody else? Yes—"

"Dr. O'Hare, since we get graded on the notes we take, can we print them out or do you need them to be handwritten?"

"I prefer..." said Professor O'Hare, whose heart began to break. It was another class that seemed to touch no one. She was not usually someone to be discouraged, but today's lecture might be her last at the university. The young dean had appointed new administration in the English department that seemed to strip away all the dignity in learning. A few of her colleagues were transferring to other colleges, some were retiring. Dr. O'Hare was afraid that the cohort of professors who embraced the classics and truly understood authors was coming to an end. The new age asked for the department to transition to a contemporary focus. It was a direction that she felt had nothing to do with literature.

"I prefer whatever works best for you. If you like to take notes on your tablets, this is okay with me. Handwritten works too. Great, um, great question."

"Cool," said the second student, who signaled toward the TA to remind them to give him participation points for his latest contribution.

"Thank you, class—"

"I have a question," said Andrei. But Professor O'Hare seemed to have already fallen in the rain.

"Please, sweetie, you can go ahead and just e-mail me. Okay?"

Andrei saw her descent immediately and so impaled her:

"Dr. O'Hare. I think you look strange," said Andrei.

The class jolted awake and let out an explosion of giggles. The chuckles came in two waves. The first wave was a genuine response from listeners. The second wave was an affectation from drowsy students who wanted to communicate they were in the same room as the professor. Dr. O'Hare only heard their large amusement and blushed, embarrassed. She held her notepad still.

"And I think you know that. And it gets in the way sometimes of your teachings because no one wants to listen to someone who looks like you. And the only way a person can survive never being listened to is if they love what they talk about. So thank you. You seem like a person that doesn't waste time on things you don't love. And that's my question. What's your antidote? How do you spend your time?"

Professor O'Hare looked at Andrei, wide-eyed, the way a newcomer stares at a fortune-teller who accurately announced their past. And for a moment Andrei's reading scared her, plus she was not used to an entire room looking straight at her all at once. Dr. O'Hare turned down his question promptly.

"I'm sorry, but my personal life has nothing to do with this lecture."

"I think it must."

O'Hare looked at this unfamiliar student in the front seat. His eyes flared with fervor. Andrei's vitality registered in her mind. No student of hers had shattered the professional crust that she hated in academia, those overly civil exchanges of ideas too safe for real opinion. But now, she felt an opening. He targeted Professor O'Hare, who, for most of her career had tried to give real answers to fake questions.

"My antidote… is to constantly create a world for me and stick to it. I don't go out much. When I do, people start planting thoughts in my head that I don't want. I would go home and think their thoughts. Bad seeds… unimportant seeds and I lose my streak of knowing what's true. That's where I'm at. I've this need to be sensitive to my inner voice. And what feeds that are movies I like… the book I'm reading… some paintings. Instead, when I am with others, my mind is occupied with repetitious jokes, and their envy, and ego. My antidote is the equivalent of a cozy castle of reality—protecting things and people I choose. A customized balance of my favorite worlds."

"That's great," replied Andrei. "A castle. That we dress. But it can sound obvious. We all do that, no? We wear band T-shirts. Put posters on our wall. Wear jewelry. Everyone customizes their reality."

"That very well can be true, um…"

"Andrei."

"Andrei," she repeated, before continuing. "But do we wear identities before having found them? Much like jumping to pretty things, as opposed to needing them. It's like wearing medals you found for sale, rather than having run the true marathon. Our preferences are innocent decisions, really, but if decided too early, can be a huge mistake. Do you see how that causes issues? People presenting themselves as people they are not? Then some people genuinely fall for their illusions, and both people lose out on something immaculate. So the posters and T-shirts and jewelry—I think all of it must be *found*. They must be needed. And it might sound dramatic, but it's the way: at one point, all of us must be lost in a desert. It's an excellent sanction. If we never have that trial, I struggle to see how else we can find ourselves."

And while she spoke, a group of various students picked up their pens and powered on various technologies to write down Professor O'Hare's words. *This relates perfectly to an essay on identity I have to write for PHIL340*, thought one student. And another: *I can use this answer for that interview I have next week.* This unfortunate phenomenon happened throughout the professor's career—the students, who could not bear natural interest in the lectures, profited off O'Hare's passion. They rested their fangs on her neck and used her original elixir for their needs. If they did it unconsciously, then another phenomenon would occur. The students imitated their teachers. And it was the largest robbery of education.

By using the vocabulary of their passionate elders, young, ambitious minds convinced themselves and the world of something they did not believe in. Articulation was so personal. It was the result of countless experiences, people, readings, and reflections. When expressing an authentic belief, some ears were fooled by the speaker's passion, which was like a contagious trance. So those ears applied others' articulation as their own. By seeing O'Hare speak enthusiastically about a topic, one, with enough attention, could easily think they loved the topic, too.

This robbery was most prevalent in art. Every artist loved their art for the same reason, and this caused no suspicion to the world. They regularly say: "My field captures the human experience." *And what is the human experience to you exactly?* questions O'Hare. "I want to be a storyteller who inspires and expresses their imagination." *But how does your chosen art differ from other mediums?* questions O'Hare. "I am a quiet observer who innately loves philosophy." *But here you are screaming this in a room,* cries Dr. O'Hare. "I am beyond grateful for the people I've worked with who made this the greatest collaboration I could have ever asked for." *But how did you collaborate—with thought and rehearsal?—or did you just perform some damn thing and sign both your names on it?* asked O'Hare.

But this phenomenon of dishonesty did not prevent O'Hare from voicing her true thoughts. She continued, with joy and vigor, to speak her heart for two reasons. The first was that by saying what she knew, she opened the door for others, hearing the noise, to walk inside and meet her there. She may meet someone who loved something the same, but for a different reason she had never heard of. Or she might perhaps learn a new thing in general—a fact, a recommendation, or something as small as a little trivia, and she adored trivia. Hope was what got the scraggly, plain-looking woman through. The second reason she continued teaching was that she knew the arch of self-denial. People would imitate her passions for their own needs and O'Hare could do nothing to stop that. Although eventually, those young people, who might be clever, quick, and able-bodied, would be asked in their field to accomplish something enormous. And within that enormity, they would fail. Their hands would shoot up to reach some place, moisten with sweat, and they would slip on the foundation of their own lies. They would have to face the truth—that when their will was asked for, their will did not show up. All they had were irrelevant strengths and old quotations from people who had the will. And if by some chance, these young people were never asked to do something enormous, then this mistake would poison them much later in life—much more deeply and sadly. They might be drinking at a bar after a promotion and wonder why they could not care. Tears would salt their bourbon and if the taste of the drink could say its name, it would call itself: *I have never loved this.*

The bell rang.

The classroom shuffled out and Andrei, looking around, found the abrupt acceptance of class being over so impossible. He frowned with difficulty at everyone's quick transition. He felt something crack in the room. It was like the feeling an artist got when he closed up his gallery, walked upstairs to his living quarters, and stared at the window to watch his former crowd rush to party next door and forget his exhibition one martini at a time. It was like goodbye. There was an unsaid, incomprehensive quality of unfairness to endings. They lacked a transition. The guitarist's identity, for example, was in her strumming ten seconds ago, not when she finished and looked up at the seduced crowd as "her" again. The singer's heart was housed in his lyrics, not in his thick-accented voice that rooms never understood.

As the lecture hall casually emptied, Andrei watched O'Hare close her notes and pack up.

Dr. O'Hare stared fixedly at her binder and seemed to read something. Andrei narrowed his eyes. The length of time in which she stared down, combined with his familiarity of that timing he had indefinably recognized throughout his life, had given Andrei sense to say to himself, *The damn lady is staring at some blank page intentionally!* And smiling at her self-sculpture, Andrei let the moment play. Dr. O'Hare continued her performance until one special moment allowed Andrei to further deepen his anchor of trust for their non-verbal communication. The professor's wrist, which lay at her side, reached up to the paper with an involuntary flick that twitched amidst its stride. *That hand! She's nervous,* he thought. *I must follow that hand.*

For O'Hare, she was no longer interested in justifying her emotions or wants. At this point in her life, she felt no shame for liking or disliking things or people. O'Hare loved thought but was committed to the power of allowing life to run. That permission led her to want Andrei to come up and approach her podium.

And by the time she looked up, he was there.

And it was extraordinary. Both of them laughed—not out of common nervousness—but because they both were tickled and delighted by the other having read their unspoken language. Their stomachs rose and the two felt happy to be in each other's presence. *Oh, so you heard me,* her smile said. *Of course, I did. You knew, too,* said his.

O'Hare looked at Andrei—seeing first the tiny holes on his cheeks, imprinted from acne scars. But his eyes were so active that they were the only thing she could focus on. He was shorter than her by a couple of inches and Andrei's sweetness and youth aided his handsomeness. To Andrei, he could see all that was unpleasant about her face—her large nose and bony frame. But inside her, there was so much peace and contentment that somehow, she lit up everywhere. Viscerally, she was beautiful to him. It was the kind of attraction between people who were really people—and who could see the other person's aura and makings. He saw what made her flesh move, and not her flesh. The intricate mechanics of her person, and not her shell. Fascinatingly enough, O'Hare saw Andrei's comet—a fire in him, a little scattered, but clearly and strikingly original. And Andrei looked at O'Hare and saw something genderless—a kind of organism that was born and that over time has been affected and affects—that was ultimately kind and brave. It was the highest rank of physical desire one could experience. When the beautiful made standard love to each other, there always lay at least one angle of ugly—maybe in the dark, from the side, with a sound they made, or everything once one was finished. In what O'Hare and Andrei shared, beauty could take its time and no second could stop it. It was the type of wholesome love that made a couple stare for minutes at the other, not because they adored their lover's eye color, but because in those minutes they were speaking to the person within the person, finding them, seeing them see, and playing together in that invisible planet created by two intuitive inventors.

Not much was said afterward. Andrei offered to accompany her down the hall, so they went. He offered to carry her books, but she preferred to hold them. That routine was hers. And their arms would rub against each other as they walked, saying almost nothing.

Andrei went into her office—neither of them had ever done it in an academic setting. They initially felt uncertain how to proceed, but of the other, they were very sure. He wanted to bite her nose and she wanted to grip his cheeks. They moved toward the person they liked and did all that was meant to be done. They kissed with unmistakable character. O'Hare had mastered English; mastery in any field defined one's behavior. When one let something kill them enough, that essence shaped their core and the person became distinctive. It gave rhythm to their kisses. Motivated their periods of intensity and retreat. How they pulled each other's hair.

And it was not "they"—the shells and bodies that were—but *they*—the spirits they found in each other. Those spirits' eyes would well up because they felt so lucky to have met one another. It looked sad, to the outside eye, two people crying as they fucked, as if atrociously forced. But it was divine.

Andrei pressed his lips over her moles, island by island, star by star, and ate them like chocolate chips. They looked at each other. He had known this all would happen because of the time in which O'Hare had stared at her paper. *And the wrist!* he said to himself. *The wrist that flicked twice without thought and I knew that wrist would be mine.* He took her wrist and sucked its skin. And he sucked it until he got out what he wanted. He held it close to his cheeks and kept it there. People did not believe in wrists, nor happenings from things like wrists, but life could go so far should one ever follow what they saw. O'Hare, too, had known this would happen the second she'd looked up from her prop of a binder and seen her other actor standing there. The lines had been said and now the stage directions were being set out. It would be the most glorious play performed by O'Hare and Andrei, that they would remember forever.

The professor gazed at Andrei and let out a thought.

"You look like you've seen something," she said, looking into his slow eyes and behind his zeal, caught the remnants of static. "What did you see?"

"Your office," he smiled. "It's messy."

The two laughed. Andrei was surprised he joked. Some strangers unlock parts of people that they never knew were inside them. Andrei did not believe he had a little humor in store—but it was always there, shrouded until the proper gust—alive because all that time before, she was her and he was him.

"Very messy," he added.

Then O'Hare shot out her funny arm and swiped a stack of essays off her desk. There was something so sudden about her movement, and the flying pieces of paper that hung in the air, that wiggled both their stomachs into a deep laugh. There it was again, another concealed doorway to life opened by an unknown gatekeeper. It was an uncommon laugh; people as a modern whole tended to laugh intellectually, at words, and the placement of words, but what Andrei and Dr. O'Hare found so hilarious was a response to the physical—to what was in front—which birthed an ancient laughter—like baby brothers pulling their father's chair from under them or soldiers waking up their comrade with a bucket of cold water. The two laughed that old roar, that was moving and universal, and found in the young, in a few underdeveloped countries, and now, in an English professor's office.

Their opening night would be their closing. In their looks, lying naked on a black rug, they threw each other flowers. And O'Hare, who, ironically a lover of diction, promised to herself never to justify in words or explanations anything that happened, did not break that rule. She merely smiled at what was a complete experience. Andrei went forward himself. He put on his clothes, not to run, or God forbid regretfully, but because it was time to put on his clothes. And she said goodbye to him and closed the door, not to pressure the inhabitant to evacuate, but because doors would not be doors if they stayed open, would they?

When Andrei left, O'Hare kissed the rug. And obscurely, Andrei walked down the corridor, lifted his hand and clutched the air in front of his chest, as if grabbing a part of his spirit, and privately threw it in her direction, saying, "Here's some of my soul forever, somehow, yes, for you."

And the two little ants trailed on their promenades.

15
THE ALLEY

Andrei's trail followed Le Conte Avenue. The sidewalk was seasoned with fallen face masks from years ago, sorority flyers, infested couches, and broken drawers people gave up on. Beside a row of scooters lined up on the edge of the street were passing cars that drew near Andrei one second and far away another. It was as if the machines were always reminding pedestrians of the direction human beings moved: "Hello! I'm coming close to you. Here. Going now. Goodbye." Andrei turned at Broxton.

The reality of life on sidewalks is it was a lot easier to imagine grandeur than to actualize it. There was no ceremony to any given second. There were patches of gray concrete. Moving machines. People who looked impossible to interrupt. So much unconquerable space in the air. It was as if an alien species dropped a smoke bomb poisoned with monotony and anywhere a man goes, he suffocates in idleness along with every element in his immediate universe. The most important event to take place was the red crosswalk signal switching to green pedestrian travel. The closest chance of romance was playing at 5:30 p.m. in the theatre. Happiness was making it to one's destination without embarrassment. Nothing appears achievable to a singular, puny ghost who is not aided by alcohol, a camera team, or a cheering crowd—only more sidewalk and sky.

But this fog died in Andrei. How could it possibly live in an activated comet? Andrei looked at the world in front of him as a place that contained no possibility for defeat. He could race a car and, given enough traffic lights, might win. He could jump over the fire hydrant he was about to pass, or explore that construction site, or trip up a student driving a scooter. A life of freedom was not adventurous, but optional. Every place and everything had a possible future awaiting—a reality he could choose to participate in or not. It was why he walked with his head up, eyes scanning, and the corners of his lips pointing upwards.

The most important state was Andrei's mind. It was a terminal that saw the truth. By this time, he was capable of slicing a moment in half to reveal its kernel. Andrei's vision was a cutting tool that could pierce any material or lie. After his travels and the decisions he had made thus far, he felt in his body a certain momentum, the force he remembered Mars telling him back at the hotel. And then he felt a secret unraveling itself, which Mars must have found at some point in her life too, whispering to him: *the more forward one lives, the more lasting their force.*

It was true that if Andrei pulled aside the passerby approaching him, and sat him down on a bench somewhere alone, he would ask two, maybe three, questions that would break the stranger's answering heart in half. He could turn a casual man mid-stroll to tears and trembling. Andrei could carve into another person, without ever needing to know them, and bring out their midnight parts. Andrei's questions might have been:

Just now, what were you thinking about?
What is your heart trying to solve?
How much longer until you give up?

And the questions were not the only factor in the stranger's would-be tears. Their surrender would have been due to Andrei's new qualities, like his eyes at the time, increasingly and fiercely present, but in the shape of himself, which kept its gentle atmosphere. It also would have been the way Andrei would move around the man, pulling him closer to his own body in a completely natural sequence. It might have been Andrei's hands, that rested so patiently, like the porcelain hand of a supreme creator resting on the edge of an armrest, but that was ready to strike up in the air to kill if force was called for. Andrei was getting closer to something.

"Andrei!"

He turned around to see David, the old co-worker, jogging toward him.

"Café earlier and now here? Crazy, man! It's meant to be! What are you up to?"

"Hey, David. I'm walking around."

"Oh, sick! What a vibe! Do you wanna walk with me? I'm headed this way."

"No," said Andrei. "But thank you."

David shifted his arms and laughed. He did not expect rejection. David considered himself friendly and a young man of great energy and there could be no possible reason why anybody should deny his invitation.

"Oh, why not?"

"David…" Andrei started on an effortless admission. The comet knew exactly how he felt and did not measure his blow. It was fair this way, so he locked his eyes kindly on David and shared: "I do not want to walk with you. There's nothing wrong with that. We don't *need* to be friends. And this is okay."

"Oh. Did I…say something bad earlier?"

"Mate, it's just who you are. And who I am. I don't want to pretend that it's pleasant to be with you."

"Dude, that really hurts me that you said that, Andrei."

"What can we do, honestly, David? Lie instead? That's how it is. It can't be changed. It's nothing on you—just the both of us combined Not every person we meet is right for us. If we treat everyone like friends, nothing is earned, you know what I mean?"

"Alright, dude. Whatever. That's totally your choice, so all good. But that literally makes no sense, so."

Andrei looked down the road, which he owed, and not David, and so withdrew.

"Then let me make no sense. Cheers. Good luck with everything."

David walked the other way and scratched his head, which was a sensible head. *People like happy people,* David thought, *which I am, and they like to spend time with happy people, which I offered.* He blinked dumb. Andrei's whole argument was illogical!—and this abnormal reasoning irritated David, whose pragmatic approach to reality refused to accept that all human beings are, indeed, anomalies. David walked briskly to his errand and thought: "No. This is civilization's formula. You treat people one way and that produces a certain reaction. That is the strategy of life. We are social animals. Right? What was he talking about?" And David thought more and talked to himself, louder and louder, so that he could not pay attention to or ever hear the current strum of the earth, which sounded like the quiet wind and the whispers of instinct, where Andrei's argument was composed, where the score of humanity always hums.

Andrei felt fresh and crossed the street, eyeing the Spanish ceramic tiles that decorated Westwood Village. Squares with flowers, suns, plants, and moons, all of various colors and designs, were placed on staircases and walls as if a joyous child had run around plastering them wherever they wanted.

Andrei traced the outlines of a tile with his slow finger. It was an orange star floating in blue. The glossy, smooth clay was cold, as if refrigerated by the wind and shade. Andrei pressed his palm against the vibrantly painted square and heard a scream.

He turned toward the noise.

The shouts continued to sound at the bus stop across the street. A shirtless man wearing a backpack was going around and grabbing women, stumbling here and there, and yelling with hostility. Everyone at the bus stop backed away.

A group of able-bodied humans paralyzed by violence seemed incomprehensible. But that was the smoke bomb of monotony entering terrified lungs, lungs alive but too shocked to act. They were afraid of getting harmed themselves to rescue those who cried out in front of them. It was amazing that regardless of how much anger was in someone, the character they might have, and what adventure films they had seen, their body did not want to move when a monster ate in front of them.

Some yelled, "Get the fuck out of here!" and "Hey! Stop! What are you doing?" One person dialed the police on their phone and another was recording the scene. But the obscene drunk kept going after the helpless women, smacking their asses, and pulling them close to his foul body.

One small lady whom he grabbed pushed him back, but was carrying too many things in her arms to make much difference. She tried to run from his yells but tripped so hard on the ground the spectators thought she would never get up. But she did get up—pulled up to her feet by this man who grabbed her breasts and like a mad dog, barked in her face.

Once the man released her, Andrei ran to the bus stop and crashed his whole body toward the drunk. It was a good hit, and Andrei recovered quickly from the cement. He stood watching the man struggle for breath, wriggling on the floor like a bug turned on its side.

When the drunk got to his feet, Andrei eyed his face and knew instantly it was not alcohol that drove this man wild. The man did not smell strongly of anything. It was another drug—one that helped saliva hang off the side of his mouth, like a feral hound. He slobbered and his eyes were two spotlights stuck on the strongest setting. His hair was disheveled, and his skin was pale and wrapped around a skinny frame.

When he faced Andrei and took his stance, both of them were certain. They knew each other. They had never met, though they understood the other's will.

Andrei's spirit was unrelenting. It had been all day. And it sought to bring this man down. It was why Andrei did not blink and instead set in his mind that he would crash his body against his enemy over and over until his own shoulder bones eroded. But the pale man was in a drug-induced state and from this power, he would never be crashed upon. He felt within himself that he could snap metal, climb clouds, and claw out a man's face until his fingernails scraped the floor. It was the event of a purely determined missile aimed at an unpredictable target. Each had their brilliance. Two comets, pure and impure. Both of their wills held tightly in the air— and then, the mutual forces, incapable of being stopped, started toward the other.

The pale man laughed up into the air, excited to kill. He thought it was the funniest thing to ever happen to him, that Andrei believed he could win this fight. The pale man stoked his fire by cursing at Andrei. The barefoot boy remained silent, watching this erratic man with caution. Then a fist came shooting toward Andrei's face, which he dodged, but then the pale man grabbed the boy by his throat and pushed him to the ground. This was a fast fight, as messy as any other thing in life. The pale man wrapped his dominant arm around Andrei's neck and squeezed. Andrei gurgled and tucked his chin into the crease of the man's arms and pulled down to break out of the chokehold. Once up, Andrei's knuckles soared into the pale man's jaw repeatedly. The two exchanged forceful kicks and the pale man kept shouting all sorts of wild things that Andrei tuned out. The problem came when the pale man pummeled Andrei's face in rage, who tripped and banged his head on the metal trash bin beside them.

A thump of excruciation caterwauled on the surface of Andrei's skull. He felt as if his head had been flattened. His eyes were flushed with dark stars and he covered his face as the pale man started to kick the boy everywhere—Andrei's ears, neck, and ribs. When Andrei looked up, a tattooed fist landed on his nose. He sensed a tiredness within the pale man that hadn't been there earlier; the pale man sweated and laughed, and crowned himself prematurely.

Andrei ate another punch to the nose and grabbed both of the man's wrists with each hand. The terrified people witnessing broke from their trances. To them, Andrei and the pale man looked like two kids who had clasped hands and tried to see who could push the other the furthest. But the curly-haired kid twisted the pale rascal's arms, who screamed in pain, shaking his head as if to tell himself he could still fight. Andrei then quickly let go and elbowed the man in the face. Blood spurted out from the pale man's nose. He looked terrifying. The whiteness of his skin mixed with his dark, sometimes bright, blood, looked like a stretched canvas that had received an aggressive throw of red paint from an upset genius. The pale man's blood sobered him up drop by drop and Andrei watched him retreat. He staggered down the street and left.

Andrei was not in the best shape himself. His sleeves were ripped, his ear was bleeding, and his head still drummed. But he'd beaten the criminal and sat under the bus stop.

He breathed calm breaths.

A mother watched Andrei as he lifted his scarf over his ear to stop the bleeding. She frowned sadly. She hated that this poor boy, young enough to be her son, could involve himself in something so stupid and minor as a mad druggie's afternoon. She pitied him and rummaged around in her purse, looking for napkins to offer Andrei. All she found were feminine hygiene products, so she opened up a pad and gave it to him. He lifted his hand, accepting the pad from the stranger. And once they locked eyes, brown on brown, she saw altruism in his comet, and the woman understood, immediately, with a human wisdom unpopular to accept, but too ancient to ever go away, that the fight needed to be fought.

The mother saw a little animal protecting the weak. And that little animal was small but ferocious. And its dark eyes when looking up at her sang their own song that she listened to be completely true to itself. Whatever he would do, she could not argue against that honest song. Had he not stepped in, no other man around would have stopped the violent aggressor. She knew that there were days in the world when one could not come home in one piece. That fights must be fought when there was nothing left. That blood, like water, has its own purpose and flow. The bus came and she climbed on, took window seat, and watched Andrei lean his back against a dirty Hollywood movie poster until he was too tiny to be seen.

Andrei sat alone. His body ached in certain places, but adrenaline had saved most of him. He held the pad to his ear. Once the material was more red than white, he went up to the trash can and tossed it inside. There was something disgraceful about the sight. He looked at his blood and felt that his dear, ruby mortality did not properly pair with crumpled canned sodas in a black plastic bag. Blood deserves an indestructible vial and an entire moon dedicated to its personal dwelling. It deserves, Andrei thought, to stay in the body. As the crimson dried and his eyes wet, he heard an argument a few yards from the stop, coming from an alley. He tuned in and identified two voices.

"Because, baby, he's dumb. Who gives a shit? You're good," said a deep voice.

"But you're my boyfriend and you just stood there," cried a woman.

"I fucking told him to get off you. You heard me, I was telling him."

"You're a—"

"I'd beat his ass. We both know that."

"No—listen to me. You didn't defend me! You. Didn't. Defend. Me!"

"Bro, I was going to—" said the deep voice.

Andrei then heard a loud slap. During the silence that followed, he rushed to the alleyway.

It looked familiar. It was at the back of a Korean restaurant and a hookah lounge and led to a parking garage across the street. The ground was wet with soggy cardboard boxes that had once carried vegetables and produce. Wet floor signs and orange cones were positioned on the floor like an abandoned game of checkers. Heaps of trash bags spilled out of the stained dumpsters that smelled like rotten fast food and urine. There were empty blue crates stacked up against the wall, where pipes slowly blew out fog. Andrei's dirty feet were now almost as charcoal as the cement.

Andrei watched the woman slap the man a second time, this time harder. She wept but eyed him the whole time.

"How… does that… feel?" she hiccupped in lamentation. She hated to use force but felt in deep ruins.

Once she brought her hand up another time, the man decked her. She stumbled a step back, looking at a man she failed to recognize. And once she caught sight of Andrei, he struck her again and yelled:

"The fuck you thought this was?" He grabbed her hair. "You wanna slap me, huh?" He hit her again. "You wanna slap me?" he repeated.

"I'm sorry," she said.

The young woman was scared, but this strange, obedient part of her at that moment wanted to get nearer to him. She'd tested him, but now it was time to go home. He terrified her. She wanted to get under the monster's large arms and look to it for help. While he often hit her, he was capable of sweet nights and being lovely sometimes. She wanted that part of him to return, and maybe she could bring that soft part back if she surrendered. The deep voice always commanded her. It told her what to think and what to do so that even when he caused her pain, she would look to him for pleasure.

"I'm sorry, baby," she apologized again, looking up at him.

But then the deep voice grunted and threw her to the floor. Her palms caught the impact and she cried. Now she didn't want home. She wanted her brothers. Her father. *Where are they? Why aren't they here?* she cried to herself. He was going to hurt her until she would no longer remember what for.

"Stop!" Andrei called to the couple.

And they both turned to the bloody boy at the end of the alley. She looked back at her boyfriend.

"Michael, don't hurt him! Let's just leave. If you touch him, we're over, I swear to God. I can't do this anymore," she told him. "You scare me." While on the inside the young woman was relieved at the show of help, she was more afraid Michael would beat the boy badly. And Michael could—he stood a little over six feet tall, and he was fat and strong. His hands were so large that Andrei saw the red stamp of his knuckles on the woman's face, that trailed from the top of her cheek to the bottom of her chin.

And when the large man turned to Andrei, the bloodied boy standing alone was, for a moment, finally afraid.

Something within Andrei was wounded after his earlier fight. His spirit needed some time to grow stronger after being too shaken up. There were vulnerable craters in him as he stood timorous in the alley, and he was unsure of what foundation he had. He had launched himself toward the scene, not knowing if triumph was in his cards, but absolutely needing to. Andrei could not tell if confronting this large, dark man was the wrong direction or the right. But once the woman continued her sobs, which were so obviously aged with abuse, he understood the reality to pursue. He was to walk down the alleyway, with the minimal confidence that he held, on some wavering morale, alone, and hold.

Nothing beautiful came from this. The woman got up, feeling a little safer, and wanted to calm Michael down or kill him altogether.

Andrei sensed her closing in, and he yelled with such violence and kindness: "PLEASE, I NEED YOU TO GO. DO

NOT COME BACK! Don't come back to this guy again. You really shouldn't. Please. Go!"

She made a move to leave.

"You stay right there," said Michael.

"Go," repeated Andrei, firmly.

Michael turned to the woman and said, "You want to see me fight someone, Noelle? Huh?"

And he stomped over to Andrei, who had not imagined an animal that large could move so fast. It grabbed him, lifting him in the air like a doll, and tossed him against a fuse box. That cruel throw would normally be reserved for the end of a fight as a finisher, but Michael had started here. Sometimes when Noelle looked at the beaten Andrei, she saw flashes of herself in the boy. The woman shrieked.

"Please... Noelle," moaned Andrei. And he sent the woman a piercing look telling her, *It will be okay if you just run now.* And she followed his instruction.

Noelle left the alley and went to call for help. She ran, her weak legs sprinting, and knew she would never take pain from anyone anymore. As she sobbed, the wind blew against her face and her vision began to clear. She felt how much more she could breathe when she was away from Michael—and this clarity resupplied fresh air to her lungs—lungs that could carry her anywhere and now sought help.

Andrei threw his first punch at Michael, but the large man's defending arms gave him no chance. Michael pushed Andrei to the ground. Andrei looked around him and found a plastic crate and swung it at Michael. But the bull came rushing toward Andrei, again so quickly. Michael held Andrei against a parking pole and welted his fists at his head. Andrei was battered. Smashed. He was the body bag of a large child that had lost the only thing that loved him. Andrei was his perfect outlet and Michael went about his menacing rehearsal.

There were moments when Andrei's comet flickered. He would dodge a punch sometimes, and land one of his own. He would get up faster than Michael expected. His best blow was grabbing a short metal pole, that locked the gate of a dumpster, and striking Michael in the head. But Andrei was a dying light and once Michael caught his second swing and whacked Andrei with what was his only weapon of hope, even Michael felt ashamed of hurting the broken toy Andrei was. Michael gave Andrei two more blows to the face.

As he was beaten, Andrei could feel the fight. He could sense its meaning and listen to it. There was no winning. The odds were against him from the moment he entered the alley. But the victory of his comet was in defending the woman named Noelle, which was what Michael could not do. Michael was no man. This was proven. He could stand menacingly, but nothing would speak louder than his lack of defense for Noelle. Michael was a giant and could beat most people out, but he could never walk toward an enemy bigger than him. They were always smaller. His excuses were even larger. Despite how visible he looked, he did not have the strength to rumble with an invisible opponent. Michael did not fight fights, he won winnings, winnings he knew he would have.

There were levels of courage, and victories hidden from the rest of the world and reserved only for hands that moved in accordance with the heart. That was bravery. Strength is the correspondence of thought and movement. The size of one's body mattered not, nor did the loudness of their voice, or the strength of their drugs. Boasts and trophies were immaterial. All of it was. The only thing that counted was if uncertain feet walked through certain alleyways.

And losing the fight was the alley's true victor, a bloody guardian defeating through defeat the cowardly champion who had risked nothing.

Michael heaved with catharsis and dealt more blows to Andrei's gut. He saw the boy not as a human, but as a thing that had taken his love away from him, humiliated him, was everything evil, was him. He thrashed with shame and struck the mirror harder whenever he ever tired. That was when he seized the hero's throat and squeezed the soft neck that just yesterday was drinking an aged cabernet and swallowing small, fresh fishes.

Andrei was about to lose consciousness when a police siren sounded in the alley.

16

WEYBURN AVENUE

Officer Gonzales, early thirties, was driving in his patrol car with his partner, Villalobos, down Westwood Plaza.

Gonzales was small and very physically active. He had grown up in East LA. Many people from that part of town recognized him for his performance at his elementary school's talent show. He was spectacular. The lineup before Gonzales' turn spotlighted a child juggling pencil pouches, a girl with a yo-yo, and a kid doing stand-up with biology puns. All acts were done light-heartedly since the kids did not want to risk embarrassment if they pursued something in full seriousness.

But little Gonzales walked shyly up to the piano and committed himself to performing two classical pieces with incredible vigor. Everyone was taken aback. The piano was three times the boy's size and his hands moved like supersonic spiders. The bleachers of the gymnasium towered over him and everyone capable of snickering watched—the sporty groups, the bookworms, the posses of skaters, the kids who wore college gear, and chic popular leadership cliques. Though regardless of their place in the school, each student felt they were given a gift from the boy. His after-school self. His fingers. His hours. And not many people, even the teachers, could play music. It was a talent that was common in photographs and as an idea, but rare to truly see and hear. It was as if the gymnasium had forgotten what the piano sounded like until the boy played it back into their memory. And every child there had their strengths. One of the students could dunk a basketball. The other memorized the multiplication table up to the twenties. But no one could create layered chords of intense emotion with a stringed instrument. No one sat down alone after a stupid school day to practice on black and white keys. Gonzales played music. This was his talent and it brought everyone to life. The principal even looked at the boy from behind the curtains and wished for a lifetime of safety and protection for him. *Look at all of those kids, loving him. Shocked by his flair. All those sounds are coming out of the boy! How could they? Don't suddenly die, please. Your talent is needed,* thought the principal. Officer Gonzales was alive and he played the piano some afternoons for his daughter. He would often work the keyboard at the station before meetings, where his partner, Villalobos, would sing happily along to his chords.

Villalobos had always been eager to work in law enforcement. When he was in high school, he assembled a group of boys from all grade levels and invited them to his house every Wednesday. Villalobos' club revolved around hunting down fugitives on the F.B.I.'s *Most Wanted* list. He led weekly research presentations that narrowed the list down to felons who were suspected to be within fifty miles of their vicinity. Villalobos held exams for his club members, testing their knowledge on how to react if they caught a criminal. He also trained them to identify what the criminals looked like with certain disguises and how to predict their next crimes and behaviors. All the boys were into it. And they trusted their leader. The amateur intelligence squad never caught any top criminals but inadvertently located the whereabouts of several robbers and proudly shared their intel with their local police station.

When Villalobos joined the police academy and became an officer, he was fulfilled. But after that fulfillment, he needed a place to go. He did not find that place until smartphones reigned over all acts of life. Villalobos made videos about his police career and became somewhat famous on social media. He would record himself putting on his gun belt, or show the world what was inside his police vehicle, and other quick fun curiosities people requested. Some of his stories and vlogs went viral and he enjoyed the attention. He looked more forward to what surprise he can catch on camera than being attentive to the needs of the community he served.

Eventually, his ordinary duty as a provider to his family was muddled up into the obligations of an internet celebrity. Society was inspired by celebrities, folks who naturally wore the best clothing, applied the most expensive makeup and ate at the fanciest restaurants. And so these areas of life were how users of social media apps spent their sparse paychecks. His salary as an officer was never enough to begin with. Nevertheless, by indulging in his newfound stardom and embracing the infinite pleasurable trends of the internet, he adopted the tribal standards of the rich. This disparity steered his judgment backward. He could either record a vlog of what was inside his police car for millions to see or look up, pull over, and show one kid on the street what was inside. He could approach a homeless man on video and give him cash or he could simply have a conversation with the camera-shy veteran who lost his home. The great thing about the internet was its access to information, but in the end, people remembered what happened to them on sidewalks.

His fans imagined Villalobos was the hardest-working officer in Los Angeles. Though while a great man and quite dutiful before his fame, his performance grew considerably weak compared to his fellow officers. People could look like anything. Any person with a phone managed their identity through a selection of photos whose appearances were impractical to debunk. One could reap the impression of a character if they pleased. People could post to appear like-minded, tough, the best, smart, creative, melancholy, and rich regardless of their actual state. A profile was a catalog of identity theft: books made one dreamy. Luxury made one wanted. Art made one complex. Travel made one busy. And minimalism made a person seem above it all.

And the pursuit of this fraud only produced further unhappiness. Users' contributions to the internet proceeded to tell the world that they were content and did not need love, while the very act of posting such a statement said that they were unhappy and indeed in need of love.

Villalobos was on his phone and checked the metrics of his latest clip.

Having just eaten, the two officers were in the mood for discussion. Both wore shades until Gonzales took them off mid-sentence.

"—almost like we're too damn smart for each other!" said Gonzales.

"That could be true." Villalobos nodded.

At the light, Gonzales came to a stop. He searched for an answer to his heart in the license plate of the car in front of them. He frowned. Nothing.

"I go on another one of those dates where it all goes good," continued Gonzales. "We like each other, it flows. We're mature. The same age, we've been around the block, right? But in the middle of the date, it just becomes a mental joust, you know? Like I'll say something and she'll reply perfectly, kind of shyly, kind of intelligently, and I'll do the same, you know, pretending like I'm confident about some opinion, and nothing comes out of it. It ends there. We just spend the whole couple of hours able to grasp each other's ideas and respond perfectly, but it's so careful that we don't get anywhere. I don't know why that happens."

"I feel you man," said Villalobos. The sun got in their eyes, so Gonzales adjusted his visor. "Everyone's different," said Villalobos. "And we never know. It's impossible."

"It's shit," sniffled Gonzales. "It's cheating. It's like we could be so smart with each other that we'll talk about feelings…Without. Ever. Feeling. But you can't call it out— it's fine on paper. But you know it isn't fine when you're sitting in your car after the date and your head is throbbing. Does that make sense?"

"I get you," said Villalobos, not getting him.

There was a respectful quality to Villalobos that Gonzales found unnerving. Everything Villalobos said was rehearsed, and while sounding genuine, Villalobos always came to some same, general conclusion regardless of the conversation. Gonzales was struggling to get somewhere with someone who was stuck somewhere in another place. Some self-help book or charisma tactic. Gonzales' partner was so convinced of an idea, something resembling empathy, that he could never diversify his thoughts to new conversations.

"We sat down to eat, right?" continued Gonzales. "And so… yeah, we sat down to eat and then we talked about chairs. Chairs! That drove our conversation gooooood. And none of us wanted to talk about it, but we smiled and made the best of it. Said a bunch of smart things about chairs—and French café chairs, and shopping for one, and sofas and her thoughts on the proper cushioning. And it was very engaging, but why didn't any of us cut the crap and say, 'I don't care about chairs. I want to— I don't know—roll around in the grass with you!' We got love all up in our heads, man. We articulate who we are, but we don't show people. She and I are just clever. There's no chemistry in being clever. I mean, why interview on dates man? It's not like anyone's gonna tell the truth. Better to lay down with her, like cubs, really be with her, and see if we want to hold each other or not. But you can't ask someone to do that, huh?" said Gonzales, defeated.

"Hey, I get you, man," assured Officer Villalobos. "And what you feel is totally valid—"

"—for Christ's sake, can you stop saying what you think you should say?" said Gonzales.

Silence ensued.

Villalobos blushed. The officer felt as though he'd been caught committing some crime. A crime that he'd hidden from himself.

"I'm sorry, bro, but all year I've been talking to you, V, and you say the same goddamn thing. It's like where'd you go?"

"Where'd I go?" asked Villalobos.

"Yeah. You're not…" Gonzales paused. "You used to say your mind; now it's all postcard shit."

"I'm sorry, man. I, uh, hadn't noticed."

"My bad, Villalobos."

"No, you're good. I mean… you're right. I'll have to think about it."

The two officers then received a call of domestic abuse and a fight by Broxton and Weyburn Avenue. Two males in an alleyway. Gonzales responded to the report and turned on his siren.

"Here we go, buddy," said Gonzales.

"Left, left!" instructed Villalobos.

Their patrol car rang its loud, urgent track and the partners conscientiously searched the column of alleys on the block.

"Damn bastard. Hitting his girl," said Gonzales. "You got eyes?"

"Nope."

"Let me know—OUT OF THE WAY! MOVE!" Gonzales honked his horn at a sedan.

"Fucking hell," said Villalobos, eyeing the vehicle.

Gonzales pressed on the gas and darted his eyes at the passing buildings. Florist. Smoke shop. Falafels. Pizza parlor. Hookah lounge.

"Right there—" said Villalobos, and the two pulled over.

The officers rushed to the center of the alleyway.

"Holy shit, he's killing the kid," said Villalobos. Michael stood like a mammoth and Villalobos worried that this aggressor was too big for him alone. He went to take out his taser, but was shortly stopped.

"No, no. You and me—let's go," said Gonzales. "HEY!"

Michael did not respond to the shouts behind him. The officers grabbed his arms and wrestled the man to the ground. Once Michael saw they were police, he stopped his brawl and allowed the cuffs to lock around his wrists.

The coward had no reason to fight the police. Meanwhile, Andrei limped away.

His eyes were wet, like a receipt machine that prints paper pain. His wounds soaked his shirt merlot. His mouth leaked like a broken faucet. The left side of his face bruised as if someone had laid his head flat and dropped truck tires on them. His ribs felt like a bad science project made of toothpicks. Andrei staggered up Hilgard Avenue toward the church and by the time the cops turned around to seize him, he was gone.

"Where's the kid?" said Gonzales.

17
THE CHURCH

In the center of the church was a purple velvet rug, lined like an artery. Its muscle was a stretch of penny wood and candles. The umber pews lined themselves up to twelve, two rows each, the left and right ribs. It was a Catholic establishment. An empty valve. Andrei pushed through the atrium whose groaning doors echoed within the chamber as he dropped to the floor.

Clinging to the ground like a little vein, Andrei looked up and saw Christ.

He saw Jesus' contoured body nailed to the cross—the lines of his abdomens and biceps stretched out beautifully, like a sorrowful ballerina reaching for the ends of the earth. Andrei gazed at Christ's head, down as if hopeless, but tilted as if there was still something left to love. Then Andrei ached and, squirming, faced the tall, walnut ceiling, and finally let go.

The church smelled of roses, incense, beeswax, and tears. His sprawled position relaxed his bones. Andrei flattened his aching back and could feel cells repairing by the minute. He took deep breaths and closed his eyes. Once calm, he rolled over to his side, brought his feet up to his chest, and hugged his knees. The wounded infant removed his jacket. He blanketed the blazer over his quivering body and napped adjacent to the crucifix.

The church was still. And fell asleep with him.

He dreamed of shapes. His head pulsated and when his eyes were shut, he saw colorless blocks fitting themselves into other blocks. He felt the sensation of a puzzle being solved and thought in numbers: *Four, eight... yes... twelve... sixteen.* Then there were periods where he simply saw the orange curtain of his eyelid. Occasional markings and former sun prints decorated his inner film with tiny dots and incoherent geometry.

Then he dreamed of his mother and said to himself, "I've gotten it wrong." He always tried to grasp life by zooming out. That was his generation. They were fast with science and believed in the cosmos, and conceptualized reality in academic comfort which made them superior to it. They argued life had no meaning and said things like, "We're just smart animals on an uncaring rock." But at some point, a person trying to organize their life with reason would be stuck in infinity. There was nothing to reason with. And so they had to return—return to the monotony that meant something a second time. "My mom," he dreamed, "once cried to me when she saw a bird chirping on her fence... real, bucket tears. She used to tell me her dreams which always meant something... A grown woman who used to pick up sticks she found pretty and keep them in her bag...She was always sweating..." There was a dumbness to her he could never understand. Andrei's mother, so pathetically an earthling, lived in touch with humanity, and was involved in it so deeply that no intelligent, zoomed-out mind could ever comprehend. "I don't want concepts. There is nowhere else to go in life except toward each other."

Last, he dreamed of the places that awaited him. He could not identify the countries. Nor the people. But they were there. Holding things. Waving. So many...

Andrei's eyes blinked slowly to life. He levered himself up with the help of a pew and carried on. He hobbled, hugging the side of the church toward the wooden statues before him: Mother Mary, Joseph, and a few saints. He approached a vast panel of wood engraved onto the wall. The woodcarving featured a portrait of Christ bleeding on the cross, centered between two other crucified men. Underneath, the inscription read:

"VERILY I SAY UNTO THEE,
TODAY SHALT THOU BE WITH ME IN PARADISE."

Andrei continued toward the front of the church. At once, he saw a table of votive candles, placed before an enclosed glass case featuring a statue of Mary. The row of lighted candles was beautiful, and so too were their heads that carried little shivering flames. The flames cast large moving shadows on the wall of infinite and unpredictable shapes that never returned to their original. Attached to the charcoal table was a beaten tin box labeled: *Intentions. Fifty cents.*

There were approximately forty candles lit and Andrei scanned through the flames, imagining what possible dedication each one had. Andrei did not believe in prayer or in God. He'd frequently passed this church over the years but had never been inside. To him, it was purely a grand building with exquisite decorations, where people did their own thing. He had no reverence for God or the devil—the Bible was just another book, the holy water was good to splash his face with, and the area in front of the altar was an ordinary space that did not call for genuflection. And so he looked at these prayer candles quite indifferently, and feeling an impulse to shape his lips into an 'O' and release some air, Andrei blew the entire table out.

One blow.

Two blows.

Last one.

Out.

Once he'd finished, large clouds of slow smoke spiraled into the dark air, for a moment appearing like fossils, and then rose into oblivion. But oblivion was not beautiful. It met him with dread. The candle blower looked back down at the black burnt tips he'd made in the waxed jars and his throat tightened.

Andrei's chest hollowed and his breath missed a turn. Something was wrong. Whatever he did was wrong. *I did that,* he gagged. He initially found the candles to be mere objects, but seeing them all revoked of purpose, and knowing he himself had changed the once collective light on the table, he felt as if he'd killed something. Forty somethings. *But how can I murder fire? It's just fire. Right?* He grew shameful. The church was so quiet that Andrei filled the silence:

"That was a mistake," he confirmed aloud.

And he worried. Andrei could hear the whispers of desperate folks who lighted their single candle to pray for relief. He heard screams for help, answers begged for, and pleas for private miracles. He'd slaughtered every single prayer.

"Where do their lights all go—now that I've done that?" asked the panicked boy.

He took a step back, surprised at his confusion. Maybe God was not real, and maybe those were just candles, but Andrei was certain of the burst of guilt cramping inside his chest for having blown out their wishes. It affected him. He would not have felt the way he did if there was nothing there. The candles were made of something, he seemed to understand, but he did not know what, only that it was a realm above his own.

And feeling apologetic, he attempted to reverse his actions. He ran up to the table and his shaking hands searched for a light.

"Where's the light?" he screamed, frightened.

He plunged his fingers into the compartment of flammable sticks, searching the crowded chamber. He could not see.

"Oh God... Oh God!" he said.

All he found in the bottom was dried wax mixed with ash. He looked around for another candle someplace else, but mass had ended that morning, along with the fire. He searched the podiums and returned to the table to try and look underneath. Then he saw the long neck of a utility lighter poking out from the right side of the stand and seized it. He began to relight the table.

One by one, Andrei dipped a drop of fire into each glass cylinder and said, *"For you and what it was… for you and what it was… for you and what it was…"* until all intentions were filled. He did not feel his sin was restored, but it was the only repair he could make. Then he got on his knees and wished for all of the previous intentions to come true, or at least make their way up to the decider. He kissed his fingertips, rubbed them on the table, and walked away.

Andrei closed in on one final statue, on the opposite side of the church.

It was of baby Jesus, standing by himself—a mature-looking child, adorable and dignified. His cheeks were carved so round and well that Andrei brought out his thumb to rub them and was disappointed by the hardness. He looked down at baby Jesus' feet and could see the etched marks of previously grazed fingers. Everyone loved to adore the feet of statues. And Andrei could see why—baby Jesus had adorable toes.

Andrei turned back at the older Jesus on the cross, hanging from the ceiling, and looked at his feet that were nailed. There was something about feet that never aged. Even with a little hair, feet seemed the body part of human beings that lived unblemished and pure. Their evolution had not gone far from what they were before, growing merely in size and always coveting that soft layer of perfect, glistening skin wrapped over veins. They were a part of the body men could trust—a piece of flesh that stayed childish and weird. The heel was not only the closest contact one had with the earth, but one of the most untouched areas of the body. Few people cup their hands to hold another's heel. The heel was always away, underneath the fabric of a sock, on the bottom of one's anatomy, deep down and far from immediate openings for conventional contact such as the hands, arms, and lips. A deep impression remained in Andrei: the image of man's feet was quite angelic.

And seeing his own, he wiggled his toes that breathed in the empty church. Andrei ran his hand in between the spaces between his toes, sniffed his fingers, and exhaled repulsively, satisfied and disgusted by the impulse. He returned to the doors and saw his old blood pebble the carpet. When he felt it was time to go, nearing the exit, he splashed some holy water on his face, hands, and feet, and made the sign of the cross.

Andrei pushed the door ajar and the sun reclaimed his eyes. He turned around to take one last look inside the smoky, brown, purple place of worship and smiled. He faced Christ and apologized. As if to a friend, Andrei said:

"I'm sorry, Jesus. I have met someone and they shared with me an idea and it's divine. I live in every way now. I understand you plan for me to enter your kingdom, but I have managed to make my life here on earth a heavenly carnival. And while I have a limited time here, that heavenly carnival does not measure itself. Each room I enter, every road I walk on, it asks for me, and waits to see whether or not I agreed to it. *Did I try? Did I grab the moment?* I love these jumps and where they lead. My jumps do not take me to you. There is a paradise within myself. I thank you for letting me rest inside your house."

Then Andrei, feeling once again he could access any degree of life, returned to the carnival that was heaven and walked toward home on Gayley Avenue.

18

WILSHIRE BOULEVARD

Andrei climbed up the carpeted stairs that creaked to the third floor. He faced his apartment.

He patted the back of his leg for his house keys, but he found nothing. He must have forgotten them somewhere, or perhaps they had fallen out. His body didn't panic. The moment his fingers had brushed his leg to discover his keys were gone, he'd accepted the fact as simply as one awakes from slumber and accepts a new morning.

In an instant, he took a few relaxed steps back, and without another breath, rammed straight into the wooden door. Wood splintered out in a bang and he burst inside. He did not stay for long. Andrei went straight for his bike helmet, grabbed his armored gloves, and opened his drawer to get the gold, spare key that belonged to his '05 Triumph.

He left his busted door open. Andrei's possessions could have gotten stolen by a thievish neighbor, but there was nothing he could not steal back. He went down to the garage for his bike. Andrei swung his right leg over the machine and mounted his butt firmly on the leather seat. He dipped his head inside his matte helmet, lifted his chin, and threaded his strap through two dusty rings, weaving it securely into a proper buckle. He turned his key to the right, flipped the power switch, kicked his left foot to neutral gear, and engaged the choke. As the bike rumbled in the garage, Andrei's hands placed themselves in their familiar brown gloves like muscle memory. After a minute, he released the choke, waddled backward, shifted to first gear, then second, and rode out of the garage and onto the street.

The biker launched smoothly ahead.

Once Andrei made the right turn and was on Wilshire Boulevard, he only needed to continue straight. The shore was just a few miles ahead. That was where he wanted to go. The beach. He was called there.

He picked up his speed to forty and his mind finally felt in equilibrium with his body. *This* was the speed that was sensible. He went up to fifty and time slowed to the molecule. He was in total control. And like a phenomenal animal, zooming past bright stores and stationary cars left behind, he could still read the names of the shops to perfection, even the license plates of multiple vehicles, in his passing course.

All onlookers saw was a black shadow that roared.

His knees squeezed the gas tank, and from the holes and rips torn from Andrei's earlier brawls, wind shot against his skin. His clothes rippled like boiling water. He worked the road like a bird works the sky—and his spirits were healed.

One mile away from Santa Monica, the street cleared. Wilshire was an empty boulevard. Incoming cars were held at red traffic lights far behind the lone motorcyclist who cruised toward the blue. And suddenly the motorcyclist felt ignited, that was, in the most subtle spark of need: to live in that alternate, finer side of life that was within reach and waited to be taken. It occurred to him what he wanted. And as that butterfly of chance flew past the biker's soul, he eyed it and caught the white-winged sign instantly. *There,* he said to himself, *I'll go.* And he attended to that meteoric obligation— that dear, vivacious reality unveiled by leaping humans. The biker wanted to see what a certain future looked like, and excitedly leaned back on his Triumph, released the clutch, and pushing off on the rubber footrests, leaned high up in the air to his right and threw himself off the bike. *Sssktthhh.*

The vehicle flickered furiously with tiny orange fireworks as it skidded on Wilshire, screeching down further and further toward the spectating ocean. The motorcyclist hit the ground shoulders first and tightened his core. His first roll catapulted him a few feet up the air, and he stretched his armored hands close to the earth's mat, trying to grab hold of the ground. But he did not slow. The biker slammed onto the pavement once again and continued to roll on the rutted treadmill of concrete and heard his helmet crack somewhere. Once gravity held him firm and still, the young man on his back looked up at the honey-orange sky, so large and balmy, opened his mouth to an acre and let out a scream because something needed to go.

After it went, he lay there for a few moments and stood on his feet. Having not crashed into anything directly, and despite one of his ankles that drummed non-stop, Andrei was not killed. He was mostly okay. A little laugh escaped the mouth.

"So that's what it feels like," he said. It was enough to know. *See?* he said to himself. The conductor shook his leg and massaged his injured ankle until it was bearable to walk on. The pier was close by. When Andrei approached his smoking bike, he pushed it to the alleyway between two rows of pastel beach houses. He threw his helmet and gloves in a dumpster and carried on.

Andrei used to be afraid of walking. The awkwardness of it once haunted him—that old, ancient army of anxieties would creep over his two-legged corpse as he'd tortured himself with his imagination. But there he was: eyes that wanted the truth, feet that had a place to go, and a determined body that would move fiercely in any intuitive direction that presented itself.

He had jumped off his motorcycle not to die, but to command. To see if the future still listened to his cue. The action was not of self-harm or reckless abuse. In the way a long pilgrimage reshaped how a man saw his country, this latest vehicle trauma reinforced in Andrei the possibility of possibility, of novelty, of inserting decisions into reality. He jumped to land the jump he made in his head. That was why Andrei was able to walk comfortably—because there existed no situation or speed that he could not flee or pursue at his own will. He could sprint forward like an animal at any second or choose to reverse and crawl back home. Hence, this stroller was able to walk at a normal pace and scan the world and its people wholly unafraid. There was no hindrance to the boy. Not a single prison of any kind contained him, no foreign lord or smidge of tyranny. How could one trap a person that lived on the pulse of truth? The honest and brave were impossible to catch.

To be caught was self-affliction. To misspend time, neglect the white butterfly, and turn one's cheek away, toward the lifeless, was destruction disguised as regularity. One harmed themselves in daily suicides by robbing their futures of their comet. Plainly, normality was a form of extinction. The self-induced pain lived in the tiniest of decisions but implied the most horrific choice: the one life provided to man was caged and protected to the point of torpid management.

Life was never about survival. For a long time, it was proposed that all living organisms shared a single purpose: to survive—but this was not the appropriate case for humans. Survival was all along but a secondary basis to man, while *attendance to life* was the first. One must secure something to survive for, as the cells of the straightforward body will, regardless of permission, do their job. Men do not breathe without air first around to inhale. A sailor cannot know his passion for sailing without an existing body of water. Similarly, a man can only survive if there is something larger in him that lives—not a beating heart, but a moving one. If he only "holds on," prolonging preservation and supervising health, there is nothing in that lingering lifeform to endanger or threaten. And since no system of security can defend from death's next play, there is no use in mortals wearing armor. The essence of chance had loitered since the beginning of time, anticipating a being who adhered to its expressions. The human priority is one's comet.

The children who played the Scorpion game in daycare knew the point. Before the beach, Andrei walked past a group of little boys and girls through the front window. He spectated their game. The kids were placed within a circle marked on the ground as a boundary. One blindfolded child played the Scorpion. And then the Scorpion violently tagged each student they found, eliminating the group one by one. The game would eventually end. The Scorpion would eat everyone. Andrei watched the children choose their mortal dance and run carefully in all directions. Then the circle of watchers applauded the child who won—that was, the timid, clever boy who had laid down patiently on the floor, away from the Scorpion, as still as a manhole cover. The unseen kid held his breath in the name of survival for the duration of the game. Though there was one player who moved unlike the rest. Bless that spirit who dared to dance teasingly in front of the Scorpion, inspect the circle to learn its space, had fleeting looks of love with other bugs, and was the only one to know what it felt like to belt their endangered voice in a loud, delightful cry toward the heavens.

The dancing crier was killed. But the shy, certain statue of a boy died twice.

That kid had a hell of a round, the observer said to himself.

Andrei went down the hill, approaching the shore slowly until bits of sand began to shelter atop his toenails. Andrei drew closer to the water and once there, collapsed to his knees before the falling sun.

19

THE BEACH

The beach was in its final act of a day-long party. Its celebrants slowed and the adults had mellowed with white wine brought from home and kisses they found there.

Families were heard playing at the seaside. Children's laughs trailed on the wind, changing the direction of atoms forever. Andrei's purple body flopped on the edge of the sea and he looked straight into the blue infinite.

Oh, what the ocean did to a man. How unmatched it was. One could competitively build a giant castle made of sand or even hire architects to construct a true castle by the shore made of rocks and furnish its enormous insides with crystals. Yet plop him closer to the sea and within seconds, he will yield and feel as dumb as any other measly man lost at land.

Andrei felt this ineptitude but did not take it personally. He looked with romance toward the horizon and let the ocean possess him. His eyes were wet, wide, and watered. His body hurt so much. He could begin to feel the soreness of his viral muscles spread, punishing him all over for overexertion and danger. Andrei's bruised mouth loosened and inhaled the saltwater scent of his water planet. And as easy as it was to breathe, tears rolled down his tender cheeks. This was no less than the transaction between nature and man. Beauty is known to pull out fluids from humans that surrender to it. And this one wept calmly, amidst the fresh breeze, to the force of the California coast. While Andrei knew he was not as strong as the ocean, he felt equal to it. He had earned the right to tell it: *You are massive, and I am tiny, but we are trying something similar, you and I. The same assignment. Should I come closer, I would be in your sea. But should you come closer, you would be in mine. You do wonderful. I love the way you tell the truth.*

He sat there for a while and watched the sun descend. The sun was masked with a thin veil of clouds and left the impression of a star that did not want to fight today. But as it sunk toward the sea, the sun quickly broke through to share a long sleeve of light and poked Andrei's faraway pupils with a twinkle. From this breach, he suddenly remembered Mars and her bright smile and perfect teeth. He wanted to call her to tell her about his day.

Andrei reached into his pocket for his phone. Its screen had cracked badly, but it made no difference; he'd missed no calls or messages. So really, the device was just a toy. He dialed the hotel number from memory and waited until the second ring.

"Hi, this is the Y.O.U. hotel in Beverly Hills, how may I assist you?"

"I need you to connect me to room four-two-five, please," said Andrei.

"And may I ask who is calling?"

"Husband. Urgent. Thank you."

"Of course. One moment."

He smiled. At first, he would tell Mars of the gardens. And then some of the people he met, the hospital, and save the fight for last. He would not tell her about the bike accident—or rather incident—because he did not want to worry her. *She might get worked up,* he thought. But most of all, Andrei wanted to know how she was doing. What did *she* do today? *Because if I left her in the early afternoon and she as a comet herself had all day to live, I wonder—*

"—Hi, Mr. Newman, unfortunately, your wife had an early checkout. She's no longer at the Y.O.U."

"What?"

Andrei's stomach fell. He held the phone and did not move. The waves touched his iceberg knees.

"I'm… I'm sorry?" he said.

"Um… Hi, Mr. Newman, unfortunately, your wife had an early checkout. She's no longer at the Y.O.U."

"No, I know—where did she go?"

"I do apologize, although I don't know the answer to that."

"She isn't there?"

"No, sir. In fact, Mrs. Newman's room has already been cleaned."

"Did she leave anything behind?"

"Nothing, Mr. Newman."

"Mars, right? It's Mars?"

"Yes, sir," said the hotel receptionist.

"You didn't see her leave?"

"No, sir."

"Not a note for the front desk?"

"No note, sir."

"…No notes on the reservation?"

"Nothing at all, sir."

"Thank you… Have a great shift," said Andrei, and hung up.

The sea teased him and retreated once again.

He wondered where she went—and was saddened he could not share all that had happened that day, or most of all thank her. Mars was gone. Mars was completely and forever gone.

I miss what you'd say next, he said of her.

The ocean's acoustics beat his ears.

Andrei looked down at the wet sand and watched the waves advance closer to the land then fall backward. Each proposal, the water took a new shape, like the varying flame of the candles back at the church. The ocean approached him briefly, saluted, and retired in casual speed. Its transient withdrawal marked different contours on the earth, spreading its foam in this place and that. And there it was, the universe showing mankind once again that nothing belongs. People go, places change, and time continues. All they had were their moments. And some of those moments turned into memories. And some of those memories hurt. And depending on whatever the pain was, that was what differentiated one person from another.

The shore reminded him of a Russian couple who were week-long guests at the hotel. He missed them. Back when he worked graveyard shifts, two guests invited Andrei up to their room during his break each night to take shots with him. The man was tall and wore a gray trench coat, laughed with his eyes closed, and was good-humored. The woman was blonde and loved to challenge them both. She usually wore a wool sweater that squeezed her slim arms. They sat Andrei on the couch and told him hilarious stories and philosophized. They counseled him in finance and spoke casually of sex. The topic would be neurodivergence one minute and breasts another. The couple laughed as though death was coming. The man would break into him and say things like: "Oh, Andrei, don't pretend. You're only saying that for yourself." And the lady, just as exact, said: "Did you know we always get one bed, but that's it? We don't fuck. They look at us like we do. Andrei, I know how it appears when I walk with him, especially tonight that I'm dressed like a slut. And of course, I'd fuck him, but it's too easy and that's our promise. Only work." Andrei had a wonderful time laughing and learning from the Russian pair, but after they shook hands and said goodbye, he never encountered guests like that again. Andrei would check in thousands of couples in due course, but no check-in would guarantee he would meet folks as inviting and so particularly splendid. An analyst would think that statistically there ought to be some equivalent experience—strangers traveling from different countries of the world must still have similar plans. One encounter must occur a second time eventually. But it never did. Not close. Life often functions in dull repetition, but humanity does not operate in patterns. Experiences are random to the point of them never happening again. People are different and they shift throughout space over time. Nothing may repeat. There is no one in a million. There is one in one. It was why no summer was the same. It was why some lips in history never got to test if they were good kissers. It was why Ali lost to Frazier but Frazier lost to Foreman. It is why film does not get another Marlon Brando and no music, however similar, can be compared to Debussy. To resurrect these greats is like trying to re-enter a lost dream. The shore motions toward the feet and never meets them exactly again.

The sky darkened. Before leaving, Andrei dug his hands deep into the sand, imagined Mars, and whispered: "I hope you keep going." He got to his feet, the way he had done all day, tucked his hands inside his pockets and took his first steps back to Westwood.

20

THE GARGOYLE

There once was a boy named Andrei who shivered on a roof, and sometime there later, there would shiver others—many others—never meeting and never needing to.

Andrei perched on the rooftop of the cinema and looked out at Westwood's nightlife bustling before him. He was mounted on the single, cream, stoned gargoyle built above in the corner of the theatre. He and his gothic animal breathed under the cold moon. Yes. He always felt like the moon—generally unnoticed by the world, that never minds—and navigated richly through his life alone and uninterrupted, like a ghost. Truth is an unobvious color. Those who attempt truth will never make billboards or conversations but usually sift in the background in awkward veritas.

He had tried so hard that day. His effort was equivalent to Olympians striving for championships or the courageous strides of soldiers who find a way. But they at least earned silver medals and were given applause. Where was his? Andrei stretched his soul for half a day without a second guess. He was supposed to return home after work, flood another bottle of red down his throat as he lay in bed and skim through a magazine. But his spine could no longer bear weightlessness. By choice, he turned around and had been drawn toward people, love, friendship, pain, crime, and even went to church. He had snatched moments with his reaching, gusty hand and it would have bothered one that there was no cushion on which they could lay their trembling heart, but Andrei knew the trembling heart was all there was. He was by himself. Mars could not comfort him and the said rooftop only offered the dry company of metal bins and pipes exuding smoke. Andrei looked toward the smoke, searching for a face, and found none.

He knew there was no reward for his life. It would continue to be excruciating for him to venture into the world with stakes and yet receive no friendly consolation. No audience. There were only things and him. The state of aloneness was the condition comets came with. Oh, what a hand could do! A friend! A touch on the shoulder! But this loud torment of silence would serve as the rhythm of a much larger song that played in him—the tune of ceaseless risk. The song commences at the first streak of undertaking. And the lyrics of progress are never congratulated. How could others toast to a victory they did not understand? That they could not see? Before, only a king knew what a crown did to a walk. No matter how diligently explained or even repetitiously tried on by others, the crown weighs not what its gold measures, but its bearer's battles, near-deaths, and navigations of terrain. Terrain cheered by none. Terrain open to all.

Andrei would soar the skies and come back to no one. He would defeat giants and walk away little. And he'd fight to seize the white butterfly of chance wholly unnoticed. This was okay. Mars *was* there. The ocean is. And there is always tomorrow's promenade.

So he leaned his head against the stone wings of the gargoyle and closed his soft, tired eyes, once a ghost, and now a happy one.

Kristian Flores, born "Karl Kristian Flores," (Oct. 20, 1999) wrote the book. The book was written by him. It was called *A Happy Ghost*. It is still called that. There was a place he was born, an ethnicity he had, a face and body he did not choose, some things he did in his life, but eventually came the book. This book. This is that book. His hand wrote it. The book is yours. His life happened, however it did. That man was me. But better now is that you are you. There is nothing to understand about this writer— no fact or detail, no achievement or anecdote— and if there was, it would not amount to any reward in your brief, beautiful life beating wild at this very second. Why would one's alma mater matter or award-winning win warrant worth if the chap's chapters are no good? There is no 'about' the author, there is the book the author wrote about. Take my lines, take my heart and run! This here is a novel and it is called *A Happy Ghost*.

MORE FROM THE AUTHOR

A collection of poems, short stories, & recipes.

◊ **Winner of the 2021 American Fiction Awards** in
    Anthologies
◊ "Unique and evocative... [Flores] contemplates everything
    ...[and] crackles with energy." - *Kirkus Reviews*

MORE FROM THE AUTHOR

A collection of one hundred poems.

◊ "A heartbreaking ode to life's difficulties... poignant...brilliant [and] exquisitely crafted." – *Kirkus Reviews*

◊ "Nuanced...and often **rife with the unexpected**. The subjects Flores chooses to focus his gaze on are surprising... It sits in a liminal territory that too few poetry books inhabit." – *UK's Neon Books*

◊ "Delicious and fresh... his words equal such a precise and complex feelings...*absolutely soul-shattering to read in the very best ways.*" **Writer's Digest 29**[th] **Annual Self-Published Book Awards** (Judge's Commentary: 5/5 Outstanding Rating)